PICTURES
AT THE
PROTEST

By Steven K. Smith

MB3 PRESS

For more information, contact us at:

MyBoys3 Press, P.O. Box 2555, Midlothian, VA 23113

www.myboys3.com

First Mass Market Printing

ISBN: 978-1-947881-28-0

To the "Lost Generation"
of students who were shut out of Virginia's public schools

PICTURES
AT THE
PROTEST

CHAPTER ONE

S am noticed his brother's lurking reflection over his shoulder in the mirror. "Get back, will you?"

"What are you talking about?" Derek replied.

"That's not six feet. You're too close."

"That doesn't count for us. How many times does Mom have to explain it to you?"

"I'd rather have you stay six feet away," said Sam.

Derek shook his head. "You're so weird."

"Uh-huh. Tell me that from six feet. Twelve years of your germs is enough. We should have started this system a long time ago." Sam looked back into the mirror over his bedroom dresser, trying to get used to the new pair of glasses that rested awkwardly on his nose. "Aren't you supposed to be helping Dad paint the deck?"

"We're not painting, Sam. We're weatherproofing. And I'm taking a break." Derek leaned back into view in the mirror and held back a chuckle. "They look good, seriously."

A sarcastic compliment from his brother was sometimes worse than an insult. Sam pushed the frames up higher on the bridge of his nose. The curved earpiece felt uncomfortable at the sides of his temples and on the top of his ears. He still couldn't understand why the doctor had said he suddenly needed glasses. The teacher may have been a bit blurry recently at the end of the school year, but he'd never had any trouble seeing the things that mattered.

"Mom wears glasses, you know. It's not so bad."

Sam sighed. "Great. Just what I want—to look like Mom."

"I didn't say you look like her. Although…" Derek turned to look at Sam's profile. "I do see the resemblance, now that you mention it."

"Just shut up, will you?" He picked up a pair of socks from the top of the dresser and chucked them at Derek.

"Okay, sorry. You don't need to be so sensitive about it." Derek walked to the doorway. "Besides, didn't Mom say you could try contacts if you didn't like these?"

"Yeah." Sam couldn't imagine sticking tiny plastic disks onto his eyeballs either, even though he knew lots of people wore them.

"Or you could get laser eye surgery. That sounds cool."

Sam shook his head. That sounded even scarier. "I don't think so."

"I guess you could just stand really close to everything. You know, be one of those close talkers who doesn't respect people's personal space." Derek crept so close that they were almost touching noses. "Can you see me now?"

"I told you, six feet apart, not six inches!" Sam shoved Derek toward the bed. "Just be quiet, will you? You're not helping."

Derek shrugged and plopped down on the comforter. "Technically, the quarantine ended yesterday. You don't even have to distance with anyone now."

"Better safe than sorry." Sam looked back at the mirror and brushed his hair lower on his forehead as if it would magically hide the frames.

"That's the story of your life, Sam." Derek pointed out the window toward the woods. "You know who's going to be relieved."

"Who?"

"Your girlfriend."

Sam rolled his eyes. As much as social distancing had changed some things, his brother's annoying tendencies were as present as ever. "Maybe you should make it six yards away. Or even better, six miles. Not seeing you *and* not hearing you would be perfect." Sam's phone buzzed in his pocket, but he resisted the urge to look at it.

"See, I told you." Derek laughed. "Does she like men in glasses? I'll bet she gives you a big hug to celebrate coming out of lockdown. Maybe even a—"

"How about I give you a big punch in the mouth?

Then we can celebrate your shutting up!" Caitlin was his best friend, but teasing Sam about being more than just friends with her continued to be one of his brother's favorite activities. Sam kept telling himself to ignore him, but older brothers seemed to know exactly which buttons to push to get a reaction.

Derek held his hands up. "Hey, I'm just saying. You don't have to get touchy about it. Maybe your new glasses will help you see better when I put you into the wall on the track. Dad said he'd take us next weekend if the weather holds up."

"More like I'll be able to see you clearly in my rearview mirror," Sam shot back. They'd recently watched a movie about stock car racing where the drivers kept talking about knocking each other into the wall around the track. Ever since, Derek was convinced he would be a natural. Sam kept trying to tell his parents that letting Derek watch stuff like that was only asking for problems, but they didn't seem to get it.

"Wash up for dinner!" their mom called from downstairs.

"Was that you, Sam?" Derek teased. "Oh wait, you just *look* like Mom." He leaped up and dashed into the hallway before Sam could throw anything at him.

With Derek finally gone, Sam read Caitlin's text.

Can you come over?

Heading to dinner now, but afterward? Sam typed back.

Cool.

"Sam!" his mom called again. "I made baked spaghetti and it's getting cold."

"Coming!" He put his phone back in his pocket and frowned at his reflection one more time. Maybe it wasn't so bad. At the very least, baked spaghetti was one of his favorites.

CHAPTER TWO

"Hey, look at you!" Caitlin was staring at his glasses. "I love them."

"I'm still not sure about them," Sam grumbled, pushing them higher on his nose self-consciously.

Caitlin smiled. "Well, I think they make you look distinguished. You'll get used to them in no time. Besides, they'll help you see the new history book I brought home from Mom's bookstore. I just have to remember where I put it." She pointed to their left. "Let's go in there. I was showing it to Dad earlier. I might have left it on his desk."

Sam followed her across the hall into the small office where Mr. Murphy worked as a professional photographer. Caitlin started rummaging through papers and searching the desk drawers. "I could have sworn I left it in here."

Mr. Murphy must have redecorated recently. Sam

didn't remember having seen so many framed photographs all over the walls. He stepped up to a group of photos mounted behind the desk. There was a picture of Mr. Murphy standing on the Great Wall of China, one on a mountain summit, and another in front of the Sydney Opera House.

"Wow. I didn't know your dad traveled so much."

"He used to do more. When Mom met him, he worked for *National Geographic* and traveled all around the world." Caitlin came to stand next to him at the wall of pictures. "He started staying closer to home after I was born."

Sam nodded. "Either way, it's a pretty cool job."

"I guess. Seems kind of normal to me, but I suppose it's all what you're used to." She turned toward the hallway. "Stay here. Maybe I left the book in the kitchen. I'll be right back."

"Uh-huh," Sam muttered, still caught up in the colorful images. He noticed a collection of square photographs spread out on a narrow table behind Mr. Murphy's desk. They were all black and white with thin, white borders around the edges.

As he stared down at the photos, Sam recognized some similarities between them. They all seemed to focus on several different kids, all of whom were Black. The kids looked slightly older than him, maybe even a little older than Derek. Some carried handwritten posters like the kind you'd hold up from the stands at a ball game to cheer for your favorite team. He squinted closer, but it was hard to make out all the words. In the backgrounds of the images he saw police officers, two older women, and a mother with her little kids. But all those people were white. It was hard to figure out exactly what was going on.

"Who said you can touch those?" a voice bellowed behind him.

Sam jumped, startled. He bumped into the table, and a photograph slipped to the floor. He spun to see Mr. Murphy and Caitlin standing in the doorway, smiling.

Caitlin shook her head. "Daddy, don't scare him like that. It's not nice."

Mr. Murphy raised his palms in the air. "I apologize, Sam. I couldn't resist."

Sam took a deep breath. "Sorry, I was just looking."

"You're as bad as Derek sometimes, Daddy."

"Well, maybe not that bad." Sam laughed. He picked up the photo that had fallen on the floor and handed it to Mr. Murphy. "Sorry, again."

"Don't worry about it, Sam. It was just a joke." Mr. Murphy turned the photo around and placed it on the table. "I shouldn't have scared you. And I'm digging the new specs, by the way. They suit you."

"Thanks." Sam looked back at the pictures on the table. "What are all these? I can't figure out what the kids are doing with the signs. Are they headed to a game or something?"

Mr. Murphy shook his head. "No game." He sat

down and pulled a magnifying glass from a desk drawer. "Here, take a closer look at those signs."

Sam leaned closer and held the lens up to one of the photos. "*Eye it, don't buy it,*" he read aloud. "I still don't get it."

"Can I try?" asked Caitlin.

Sam handed her the magnifying glass, and she leaned over another old photo. "*Americans do not practice what they preach.*" She looked back at her dad. "That definitely doesn't seem like something you'd hold up at a ball game. What's it mean?"

"I guess it is hard to figure out without the context." Mr. Murphy swiveled his chair toward them. "Those photos are from the collection scanned by Virginia Commonwealth University. They're part of a showcase I'm helping one of the university librarians organize. They're from student protests along Main Street in Farmville during the summer of 1963."

"What were they protesting?" asked Sam.

Mr. Murphy crossed his arms. "It's something you two might identify with, in a way."

"They had to deal with annoying older brothers too?"

Mr. Murphy chuckled. "No, something much more serious than that. Their schools had been closed down."

Sam raised his eyebrows. "Really? Was it because of a virus? Did they have another pandemic? Was it the Spanish Flu?"

Caitlin shook her head. "That was in 1918, Sam."

"Good guess," said Mr. Murphy, "but their schools

weren't shut because of a virus, although you might argue that the reason was just as bad as a disease. Prince Edward County closed their public schools for five years, and these kids wanted to go back to school."

Sam's mouth dropped open. "Five years! Oh my gosh, my mom is about to lose it if we don't go back in the fall. She'd never last that long."

"Prince Edward," said Caitlin. "That's just a couple counties over from here, right?"

Mr. Murphy nodded. "That's right. You might remember we went to a street festival at Longwood University in Farmville a couple years ago."

Caitlin picked up a photo. "But why do *you* have these?"

"I thought you just took photos," said Sam. "Do you organize them too?"

"Normally, I'm the one taking the pictures, yes. But these are special. The local police department took many of these pictures as potential evidence against the protestors. They stored the entire collection in the basement of the station. A few years ago, someone rescued them during renovations at the station for a private collection. A historian shared them for digital use by my librarian friend, Natalie Roberts, at VCU."

"If there wasn't a pandemic, why in the world would they have closed the schools for five years?" asked Caitlin.

"Was there a natural disaster or something?" asked Sam. "Like an earthquake or a flood that destroyed all the buildings?"

"Well," said Mr. Murphy, "back in the fifties, there was a big decision from the US Supreme Court called *Brown vs. Board of Education*."

"Oh…" said Caitlin, seeming to catch on.

That name sounded familiar, but Sam didn't quite remember the details. "What about it?"

"The Court said it was illegal to have separate schools for Black and white students," explained Caitlin.

Mr. Murphy leaned back in his chair. "That's right. But in Prince Edward, the county leaders—who were all white, mind you—decided that they weren't going to desegregate like the courts had ordered. Instead, they closed down all the public schools and opened a private school that only whites could attend."

Sam knew that Virginia had been part of the Confederacy and had fought to keep slavery, but the Civil War had been almost a hundred years before the 1960s. Could those views still have been around after all that time?

"That's the craziest thing I've ever heard," huffed Caitlin. "I mean, what were they thinking? America's not supposed to be like that."

Mr. Murphy sighed. "You don't have to convince me, honey, but the South hasn't always been so quick to change its ways. Virginia likes to think of itself as doing things in a civilized fashion, but it's been on the wrong side of history in a lot of issues involving race—slavery, voting rights, school desegregation, interracial marriage, the list goes on. Some folks have different views on those points, but that's how I see it."

"But even if the county leaders were fighting against integrating the schools, wouldn't the governor or somebody still force them back open?" asked Sam. "I mean, the Supreme Court ruled that they had to, right?"

"Like I said, Virginia has not always been super-fast to change," replied Mr. Murphy. "In fact, many state officials were against desegregation." He glanced back at the group of pictures and then held up his finger. "You know, I hadn't thought of this until you started asking questions about the pictures, but I could use some of that expert investigation work that you both seem to enjoy so much with your mysteries."

Caitlin raised her head. "But this isn't much of a mystery, is it? It's just a story about a bunch of ignorant people who didn't want to treat everyone fairly."

Mr. Murphy smiled. "True, but I was thinking about something more specific to do with this project with the university." He opened a table drawer and pulled out a shoebox-sized container. He lifted the lid to reveal dozens of photographs in the same square shape as the ones on the table. Cardboard dividers separated them into sections like a box of Sam's baseball cards.

Mr. Murphy leafed through the container, then he stopped and pulled out a particular section. "Here we go, these are the ones." He spread a dozen new photos out across the desk.

"What's so special about those?" asked Sam.

Caitlin leaned closer. "They look just like the other ones."

"They're from the same Farmville protests," said Mr. Murphy, "but this batch has a mysterious twist."

Sam looked up from the photos. "Mysterious?"

"Mysterious how?" asked Caitlin.

Mr. Murphy smiled. "I thought that would catch your attention. My friend Natalie has attached names to most of the faces in the collection, but no one has identified the kids in these particular photos."

Sam picked up one of the new pictures. A young African-American girl held up a sign that read, "Freedom now for all men and women." He stared closer with the magnifying glass, taking in the details of her face, her clothes, and the sign. She was marching along a sidewalk in front of a glass storefront, and a reflection of the street shone in the window. He noticed what looked like antique cars and people standing by and watching. It was a snapshot—a frozen moment in time—and there was something captivating about it.

He looked over at Mr. Murphy. "Do you really need help with finding these people, or are you just trying to give us something to do?" Sometimes his mom and dad gave Derek and him projects around the house that didn't really need doing, just to keep them occupied and out of the way. Or at least that's how it seemed. Maybe Caitlin's parents were the same way.

"Don't be so cynical, Sam." Mr. Murphy chuckled. "This isn't just busywork, trust me. Tracking down these people might not be easy. That's why I called it a mystery. Those photographs were taken nearly sixty years ago. Those kids may have been teenagers that lived in Farmville in 1963, but by now, many may have moved away, some have died, and others very well might not want to talk about it or even be identified. But I know for a fact that Natalie's looking for some assistance." He looked over at them expectantly. "So, what do you think? Can you help us out?"

Sam saw the twinkle in Caitlin's eye and knew it could only mean one thing. In all the years they'd been friends, she'd never turned down a chance to learn more about history. The mystery attached to it only sweetened the pot. He smiled and nodded. That was one of the things that drew them together. They both enjoyed solving puzzles.

"We'll do it!" Caitlin proclaimed.

"Excellent," said Mr. Murphy. "I'll let Natalie know that I've got a crack investigation team on the case. I'm heading over to VCU tomorrow. Why don't you come along and introduce yourselves? She can show you all the photos in question. I'm sure you can make copies of the ones that interest you and start your own file."

"We can get Derek to help us too," suggested Caitlin.

Sam groaned. He'd had a feeling she was going to say that.

Caitlin nudged him in the ribs. "Oh, come on. You know he's always a big help."

"He's a big something, that's for sure."

CHAPTER THREE

When Sam emerged from the path in the woods on his way back from Caitlin's house, he saw his dad's ladder perched against their elevated deck. Derek stood at the top, brushing the railing's spindles with weatherproofing. Their neighbor, Mr. Haskins, was sitting in an Adirondack chair in the grass at the base of the ladder with a drink.

"Hey, Mr. Haskins."

The old man took a long sip from the glass and wiped his mouth with his hand. "Ahh. Nothin' like a good glass of lemonade on a job."

"What are you doing over here?" It didn't look like their neighbor was doing much work.

"Supervising." He grinned back at Sam. "How come you're not up there, boy?"

"That's a very good question," Derek called down

from the top of the ladder. "I could use the help, you know, Sam."

Sam shielded his eyes from the sun and looked up at Derek. "You didn't want to split the money, remember?" Dad had said the deck needed resealing before winter and offered to pay fifty bucks for the job. Derek quickly jumped at the chance to do it himself without thinking much about how much work it would be.

Derek looked down at Sam and frowned. "I'm reconsidering."

Even from down on the ground, Sam could tell one of the wooden railing spindles wasn't shiny with weatherproofing like the others. "You missed a spot there on the left." Maybe 20/20 vision could come in handy sometimes.

"You might twist my arm to let you paint my deck too, when you're done here," said Mr. Haskins. "If I approve of your work, that is."

Derek grunted. "I don't know. My arm's getting tired."

"How much do you pay?" asked Sam. Heights had never been his thing, but Mr. Haskins' deck was at ground level. If Derek didn't want the money, maybe Sam would step in.

"Well now, I guess that depends on the work." Mr. Haskins glanced down at his drink. "I suppose a bottomless glass of cold lemonade won't be enough for you?"

Sam laughed. "Nice try."

The old man cocked his head to the side and stared

at him. "I was about your age when I got my first pair of spectacles."

"Did you like them?" asked Sam. He was tiring of everyone noticing them for the first time.

"Took a little time to get used to, but they drove the girls crazy."

"Really?" Sometimes it was hard for Sam to tell when the old man was being serious or just pulling his leg.

Mr. Haskins grinned. "Like moths to a flame. I had to fight them off."

"Sam has to fight girls off," said Derek, "but not for the reason you're thinking."

Mr. Haskins looked out to the woods. "Where are you coming from? Just a stroll along the creek?"

Sam explained he'd been over at Caitlin's house. "Her dad has a project for us. He wants us to help identify people in some old photos from the 1960s."

"Were they from Woodstock?" called Derek. "Did you go to that, Mr. Haskins?"

"Woodstock? Nah, that was a little after my youthful years. I'd already married the missus by then. But plenty of other radical things happened in that decade—JFK, Martin Luther King, Bobby Kennedy, landing on the moon, the war in Vietnam—the world felt like it was changing fast, let me tell you. And Virginia was no different."

"The pictures were of students protesting their schools being closed," said Sam.

Mr. Haskins nodded. "You must be talking about Prince Edward County."

"How did you know?"

Mr. Haskins waved his hand. "I live here, don't I?"

"Did you see them?" asked Sam. "The protests, I mean."

"No, I wasn't there, but they didn't surprise me much, either. It wasn't an easy time to be colored back then."

Sam cringed. "I don't think you're supposed to call people that anymore, Mr. Haskins."

The old man waved his hand. "I guess not, but that's what we said back then—colored, Negro, and some people said plenty worse things too, I'm afraid. My pap worked with lots of Black folk when he was a bellman at the Jefferson Hotel, but prejudice was aplenty back then with Jim Crow."

"Jim Crow?" Derek had stopped painting and was sitting on the top ladder rung, turned toward them. He seemed happy for an excuse to take a break. "What's that?"

Mr. Haskins let out a cackle. "I gotta teach you boys everything. The Jim Crow South, that's what they called it. It was what they called the laws that kept things separate between white and Black—most every public place was segregated, like bathrooms, drinking fountains, trains, buses, restaurants, theaters, schools…"

Sam shook his head. Sometimes he forgot how much

remained unfair even after slavery ended. Especially in the South. "That's terrible."

"Yes, you're right, boy. But that's how it was back then. It takes a long time to change tradition, and a lot of folks in the South were set in their ways. Still are, I suppose."

"Caitlin's dad is taking us to VCU tomorrow to talk with one of the librarians about the pictures." Sam looked up at Derek and hesitated to invite him, but he knew Caitlin would if he didn't. "Wanna come with us?"

"To the library?" Derek waved his brush at the rest of the railing spindles. "And give up all this? Are you crazy?"

Sam hadn't thought his brother would be too eager to do research at the library. He'd wait to tell Derek anything about the mystery until they knew more. "Your loss."

"And what about the go-karts?" Derek called.

"They'll still be there when we get back," Sam answered, turning to walk inside.

Mr. Haskins called out to him. "Don't tire yourself out too much with your research. My offer to paint the deck still stands."

"Thanks." Sam laughed. "I'll get back to you."

CHAPTER FOUR

C aitlin rapped gently on the edge of the wooden door. "Research Librarian" was printed in thin gold letters across the frosted glass.

"Come on in," a woman's voice answered. Sam followed Caitlin into the office. It was a good-sized room but seemed cramped by the crush of bookcases, shelves, and file cabinets that were crammed into every square inch. A woman glanced up from a book and waved at them from behind a desk on the far side of the room. "Well, hello there." She had graying, curly hair, but her eyes were bright, and Sam thought she must not be much older than his mom.

"Mrs. Roberts?" Caitlin asked.

"Yes, but please call me Natalie. My hair may be graying, but I'm not too old yet!" She stood and walked around the desk toward them. "You must be Caitlin.

Your dad told me you might stop by. And who is this young man?"

"This is—"

"Sam," he said quickly before she could finish. It might not have been his idea to come, but he could at least say his own name.

"Well, it's nice to meet you both," said Natalie. "Here, let me make some room so we can sit." She reached down and moved several piles of papers and magazines, revealing two wooden chairs. "That's better. Please, sit down." She turned a padded leather chair toward them and sat, crossing her legs. "So, your dad tells me you might be up for helping me with my research."

Caitlin grinned. "We sure would."

"I believe he described you as an amateur sleuth. Is that right?"

"We *both* like to solve mysteries," Sam answered. He knew from experience that if he didn't speak up, things could quickly turn into the Caitlin Show and leave him in the shadows.

Caitlin glanced around. "My dad showed us some pictures. He said they're part of the collection that you're working on from the sixties."

Natalie nodded. "They sure are." She reached over and lifted a rectangular box from the nearest file cabinet and then moved to clear more space on a table behind them. "Pull up your chairs. We can look at them over here."

She took a handful of square, black-and-white photos from the box and spread them out in a grid. It reminded Sam of a game of concentration, but with all the boxes already turned over. "These are all from the student protest?" he asked.

"Yes, it's part of a larger online collection, but these are the ones we want to focus on." Several of the photos had a red check on the white border, and Natalie placed them in their own group.

"Are they the ones that you haven't been able to identify the people in?" asked Caitlin.

"That's exactly right."

Sam leaned closer and stared at the images spread across the table. They were like Mr. Murphy's, except of different people. One showed two teenage boys walking together in front of a storefront. Another had a slightly older girl confidently holding a poster with the words, "DON'T BUY SEGREGATION." Like the other pictures, most everyone holding the signs seemed to be African-American, with just a few white people in the background or walking past.

"I can't believe they wouldn't let these kids go to school," said Caitlin.

Natalie sat back in her chair. "Did your father explain what was going on?"

Caitlin nodded. "Sort of. He said that the town didn't want to desegregate the schools after the *Brown vs. Board of Education* court decision, so instead they closed down the schools for five years. Although that's really hard to believe."

Natalie nodded. "Sadly, it can take a long time to break through stubbornness."

"But didn't that mean the white kids were out of school for five years as well?" asked Sam. "Even if people in the town were stubborn, weren't they hurting their own families at the same time?"

Natalie sighed. "It was tricky, Sam. While the public schools were closed, new private academy schools that were exclusively white started springing up all across the South. In fact, a good number of private schools that you might run across today have roots in this time in the fifties and sixties, even if that isn't their purpose now."

"So Black kids just stayed home?" asked Caitlin. "Were they homeschooled, at least?"

"It depends. Some were taught at home or in groups at churches. Other families sent their children out of state to learn, even if it meant being separated. But many, including some poor white students, just went without. In the fall of 1963, the Free Schools opened, but it took another year before there were any public schools. And even four years is a long time when you're a young person! Imagine if you couldn't start first grade until you were old enough to be in fifth!"

"That's terrible," said Caitlin.

"They've been called the 'lost generation,'" added Natalie, "because some of those students never did catch up with the education they missed. Some never fully learned how to read and write, which severely impacted their ability to get ahead in life."

Sometimes Sam felt like he was never going to be done with school. He couldn't imagine having to start five years late. He looked back at the table. "Why do you want to know who these people are in the pictures? They must be pretty old by now."

"It's history, Sam," said Caitlin. "It's how we learn about things, remember?"

"I know that, Caitlin." Sam frowned. He didn't need anyone telling him that history was important. "What I mean is, what are you going to do with their names if you can find them? Maybe some of these people would rather forget about what happened back then."

Natalie held up a photo. "You're both right, actually. We absolutely need to learn from history. *And* some folks would rather move on and not draw attention to what happened back then, although I've found it tends to be mostly white folks who feel that way. These pictures were hidden away for decades. Most of the people I've identi-fied have been quite moved to see the images of them-selves and others they knew from that difficult time. They were extremely brave to stand up and march in protest like that, even though they were kids. That kind of bravery doesn't just disappear. Have either of you been to the Moton Museum?"

Sam didn't think so and shook his head. "What's that?"

"It's the former Farmville high school for Black

students. A girl named Barbara Johns led a student protest there ten years before the protest in these pictures. It's become a wonderful civil rights museum. You should certainly visit if you want to better understand the history we're talking about."

"Wow," said Caitlin. "I'll have to ask my dad to take us."

"And, selfishly, it fits well into the sleuthing that you'll do for me," said Natalie, a sly smile on her face. "If you're interested, that is."

"It sounds fun," said Caitlin.

"How have you identified the ones you've found so far?" asked Sam.

"Oh, a number of methods. It's like a breadcrumb trail. I start with one person and they often remember other names and faces. We've also used county records, church registries, census cards, high school yearbooks—all sorts of things."

Sam saw Caitlin glance at him questioningly. It sounded like an interesting challenge, and he was never one to turn down a mystery. And this one didn't seem packed with danger and peril, which would be a welcome change after most of their adventures. "Works for me."

Caitlin turned back to Natalie. "Okay, we're in."

Natalie clapped her hands together like cymbals. "Excellent!"

"Where do we start?" asked Sam.

Natalie walked behind her desk. "Well, I can give you a binder with some background notes and the information from the photos we've already identified. But I suggest you start by picking out a photo or two from that group on the table. See if one catches your eye."

Sam and Caitlin stared back at the images, each its own little snapshot of history. How would they decide which one to investigate? There was no telling which would be easy and which would be challenging. Caitlin picked up one from the top row. She examined it for a few moments and then handed it to him. "How about this one?"

Sam studied the image of a Black teenage girl walking past a gruff-looking white man in a hat. He didn't seem to be paying any attention as she confidently held up a sign that read, "*Educate Don't Segregate*." She had a determined look in her eye, like she wasn't afraid. "Why that one?"

Caitlin stared back at the picture. "There's something about her expression, like she doesn't care that she's just a high schooler. Like even though the whole town, maybe even the entire state, is against her, she knows what she's doing is right and she's willing to take a stand."

Sam glanced back at the image and then up at Caitlin. "You can see all that from one picture?"

"I have a sense about these things. Just like Ellie and Nelly, remember?"

He chuckled, remembering how fixated Caitlin had become when they'd found an old journal from two of Thomas Jefferson's granddaughters. She'd taken an immediate liking to them and was determined to figure out their story. Maybe she did have an intuition about things. She was certainly a good investigator.

"I think your father was right," said Natalie, watching them from her desk. "That kind of passion and empathy is exactly what's needed in this sort of job."

Caitlin's face beamed the way it always did when a teacher or other grown-up complimented her. "Thanks."

"Okay," said Sam, "so we'll investigate this picture. But where do we start? What's our first step? This girl could be anywhere by now."

"How about Farmville?" asked Caitlin. "I mean, if we're going to figure out who she was, we should begin where the picture was taken, right? Maybe they can help us at the Moton Museum."

"I was going to suggest that very thing," said Natalie, "but I like that you figured it out yourselves. I have a contact there who's been one of my best helps in starting down many of these identification trails. She might be able to direct you to the right folks in town. The county records office is also nearby. You may need to send a few emails, make some phone calls, maybe even knock on a door or two, but I'll bet you'll find something."

They thanked Natalie and walked outside. Even though it was summer, there were still many students coming and going along the sidewalk, some carrying backpacks, others just on their way somewhere. "Sounds like a lot of work," said Sam as Caitlin texted her dad.

She nudged him playfully. "Come on, don't be like that. It's always a lot of work, Sam. But it's worth it when we solve the mystery, remember? Plus, think about being one of those kids who were locked out of school. They deserved to go to school just like everyone else. It's not fair."

"We can't exactly fix that. We can't replace the years they missed school. We're just trying to find their names, remember? It's not like we were the prejudiced ones who closed the schools."

Caitlin turned and looked at him. "Of course not. But we're the ones here now with an opportunity to make a small difference. Even if it wasn't our fault."

He shrugged. "I guess you're right."

Mr. Murphy's pickup appeared across the parking lot and stopped near them at the curb. Caitlin climbed into the passenger seat and Sam sat in the back of the truck's extended cab.

"Well," asked Mr. Murphy. "How did it go?"

"Great," said Caitlin. "Natalie's really nice."

Mr. Murphy laughed. "Oh, it's already Natalie, is it?"

"That's what she told us to call her," said Sam. "We saw more of the pictures from the student protests."

"So, she agreed to let you help?"

Caitlin nodded. "Yep. We even picked out a picture to start with. It's of a teenage girl who's holding a sign along Main Street. I can already tell we have a connection."

Mr. Murphy turned and raised his eyebrows. "Is that right?"

"She always thinks she has a connection to things," Sam muttered.

Caitlin reached back and swatted his leg. "Be quiet. You know what I mean. Natalie suggested that we visit the Moton Museum in Farmville. Could you take us?"

"We can probably work that out," said Mr. Murphy. "It's only an hour away, and I've been meaning to stop in and speak with one of the faculty over at Longwood."

"Great." Caitlin looked back at Sam. "Do you think Derek will want to come?"

"To a museum?" Museums were not much higher on his brother's list than libraries. He preferred the exciting and dangerous parts of solving mysteries over the learning parts. "He'll complain, but he'll probably come."

"You know what you could do?" said Mr. Murphy as they turned onto the highway. "The High Bridge Trail runs straight into Main Street in Farmville. It's a nice, even stretch for bike riding. I could drop you off at the trailhead and then meet you in town for lunch before you see the museum."

"That sounds fun," said Sam, knowing it might minimize some of his brother's complaining.

Caitlin glanced back at him with a grin. "Maybe we could get one of those tandem bikes like we rode at Jamestown!"

Sam shook his head. He'd barely made it off of that death-trap alive. "Don't even think about it. Once was more than enough."

CHAPTER FIVE

Mr. Murphy banged the tailgate of his truck closed in the parking lot. "You're sure you have enough water?"

"We'll be fine," Caitlin answered. "You said it's flat the whole way."

"I'll keep an eye on the two of them," Derek added. "Or maybe I should say that Sam will keep his *four* eyes on *us*."

"How would you like both my fists on you?" Sam shot back.

"Sure, but you'll have to catch me first!" Derek stood on his left pedal and then burst forward onto the trail. "But be careful, I might put you into the wall!"

Mr. Murphy chuckled and got into his truck. "Okay, then I'll meet up with you in town for lunch around noon. Call me if you have any problems."

Caitlin and Sam waved as the pickup pulled away.

"He's so annoying."

"Sam! That's so rude."

"No, I don't mean your dad. I meant *him*." He pointed to Derek, still racing up ahead like a fool. He'd run out of energy in no time at that rate. "How far is it again?"

"The entire trail stretches about thirty miles. Or at least that's what the sign said."

"Thirty miles?" Sam felt tired already.

Caitlin smiled. "But it's only six to get to Farmville where we're meeting my dad for lunch on Main Street."

"That's a little better." They started forward, their tires crunching against the light-colored gravel that was hard-packed for riding. The air was humid, and he already felt a bead of sweat drip down from under his bike helmet.

They hadn't ridden far when a break in the trees appeared up ahead. Derek had pulled off the trail and was staring over the railing. "Look at this!" he yelled as they came closer. "It's amazing!"

"Is this the High Bridge?" Sam asked as they rolled to a stop.

"Come over and see for yourself," Derek answered.

Sam rested his bike against the wooden railing. He clutched the edge with both hands before extending his head just enough over the side to see below. It was quite a view. They were up above the tops of the trees, and the land had dropped away below them into a river valley. The bridge stretched up ahead as far as he could see. It seemed to be built on an old railroad trestle, like the kind in cartoons where the bandits tied someone to the tracks just before the train came around the bend.

Caitlin nudged him playfully. "High enough for you?"

"Totally."

"Can you imagine bungee jumping off of this baby?" said Derek, climbing up on the first row of the railing.

"No," Sam said quickly. "Get down from there, will you?" There was a wire screen to keep anyone from falling through, but why even tempt it?

"Aw, relax, Sam. I think it's cool."

"Yeah…" Sam said as he stared down at the water moving over the rocks far below him. If they really were in a movie, the water below would be filled with ravenous crocodiles. "Is that the James River?"

Caitlin shook her head. "It's the Appomattox. The bridge is a hundred twenty-five feet high and was built back in 1853."

Derek raised his eyebrows. "You know that off the top of your head? Sometimes I think you just make all this stuff up. Your whole smart-girl thing might just be an act."

"And your whole stupid routine is just an act too, I suppose," she shot back.

Derek opened his mouth but didn't have a comeback for that one.

Caitlin grinned. "Actually, I just did some research before we came. I like to plan ahead before I go someplace. I don't think there's anything wrong with that. You should try it sometime."

"Yeah, yeah," mumbled Derek. "Sam looks like our mom and you sound like her."

"Hey." Caitlin put her hands on her hips. "I like your mom."

"Uh-huh." Derek took another step up the railing. "So, why'd they build this thing, anyway? Was it just for trains?"

"Exactly," Caitlin said. "But during the Civil War, General Robert E. Lee marched his Confederate Army across this bridge as he retreated from Farmville. They actually tried to burn the bridge to keep the Northern army from using it, but Union soldiers put the fire out before it was destroyed. Union forces followed Lee all the way to Appomattox Courthouse."

"They took him to court?" Sam had never heard of that happening in the middle of a war.

Caitlin laughed. "It wasn't an actual court, Sam. That's the name of the town—Appomattox Courthouse. It's where Lee surrendered to General Ulysses S. Grant to formally end the war."

"Next time you two should bring your history books along for the ride," Derek teased, jumping back down to the bridge path. "Can we go now?"

Sam leaned a little further over the railing and watched the water turn white as it flowed over the rocks. He wondered how anyone could have built such an enormous bridge back in 1853 without the aid of cranes and other modern equipment. What must it have felt like to be a soldier crossing this bridge at the end of the Civil War?

"Don't fall, Sam!" Derek grabbed him at the waist and faked like he was going to throw him over the railing. Sam reached his arm back to push away his brother's grip, but as he whipped his head around, his glasses came loose and slipped over his nose. Sam felt them falling. He lunged for them with his left hand, but his finger grazed the earpiece just enough to send them tumbling past the top railing.

"No!" Sam shouted, stretching over the railing and clutching at the air. He watched the glasses drop out of sight. He spun back around and screamed at Derek. "What did you do that for?"

"Oh, Sam," whispered Caitlin.

"Me?" The grin had disappeared from Derek's face, but he held his hands up innocently. "I didn't drop your glasses. I just touched you and you totally freaked out. Why were you leaning so far over the edge, anyway?"

"Why was *I* leaning over the edge?" Sam fumed. "Get over here. I'm going to kill you!" He leaped forward, but Derek retreated out of reach.

Caitlin stepped between them. "Okay, that's not going to help. He didn't mean for your glasses to fall over the side, Sam." She glanced down to the river. "Maybe they're okay."

"Okay?" Sam shook his head in amazement. "You just said that this bridge is like a thousand feet high."

"It was more like a hundred," Derek called.

"Quiet!" Sam growled. "They're probably smashed on a rock and broken into a million pieces. Or if not that, they probably got washed down the river."

Derek climbed on his bike and turned back the way they'd come.

"Where are you going?" Caitlin called.

"To find Sam's glasses. Where else?"

"Good luck!" Sam huffed and shook his head. Finding his glasses now seemed like a lost cause. He squinted down to the base of the bridge supports. "Can we even get down there?"

"I guess we can try." Caitlin pulled her bike away from the railing and climbed on. "Are you okay? You know he didn't mean for that to happen."

Sam frowned. "Yeah. Whatever. I hated those things anyhow." That kind of thing happened all the time with Derek. He was always messing around and then acting baffled when things went wrong. Sam preferred to live life a couple steps away from the edge to give himself a little buffer, just in case. Sure, sometimes he needed a little nudging to try new things, but life with Derek was too often like walking a tightrope. A little security was never a bad thing.

"Come on," called Caitlin. "We might find them."

CHAPTER SIX

W hen Sam and Caitlin reached the edge of the bridge, Derek had already stowed his bike and disappeared into the trees.

"Is there even a trail?" asked Sam. Leave it to his brother to charge blindly down the hill and lead them over a cliff.

Caitlin pointed to an opening between the branches. "I think he went in over there. It doesn't look too steep."

"Come on, Sam," Derek called from somewhere through the trees. "There's a little path down here. It's almost like people use it when they drop their glasses over the bridge."

Sam felt his blood boil again. "I didn't drop them. You shoved me."

"That too!" Derek shouted.

Caitlin ducked into the leaves, and Sam reluctantly

followed behind. A thin, steep path wound between rocks and trees down to the river valley. Sam turned his foot sideways and half walked, half slid along the slope. His foot slipped more than he'd expected a couple times, showering a cascade of pebbles down into the ravine. He tried not to imagine being one of those stones tumbling down the side of the mountain. All because of his stupid glasses.

"Careful!" Derek called up to them. "There's some loose dirt back there."

"Yeah, thanks for the early warning," Sam yelled back, picturing his brother's stupid grin.

Caitlin moved nimbly ahead of him, like she'd descended the mountain dozens of times. "We're almost to the bottom."

"I'm fine," Sam answered. "Just keep going." She and Derek both knew that he didn't like heights, but he was still determined not to show it too much.

Eventually the ground leveled out. Lush green ferns and tall grasses grew all around the river. A bird call broke the silence, but the air felt thicker down in the valley.

Sam looked above them and saw the bridge supports extending high into the sky, like someone had built a giant ladder in the air. "What are we even doing down here? I told you, they're probably lost."

Caitlin waved him forward. "We might as well look for them."

They walked toward the sound of rushing water and found Derek perched on a large rock at the edge of the river. "Cool, huh? I feel like a rugged explorer. I think I'll call it the Drop-a-mattox River. What do you think?"

Caitlin laughed and gazed all around. "It's like another world down here." She stepped up on the rock and stared down into the water. "Look! There's a fish!"

Sam rolled his eyes. "Rivers tend to have those." He glanced back up through the trees. How were they even going to get back up to the bridge? Climbing up would surely be harder than sliding down.

Derek crouched down and picked up a stone. "Where's that fish? I bet I can hit it."

"No!" Caitlin shrieked. "Leave it alone. It's just swimming. We're the ones intruding."

"Aw." Derek turned and skipped the rock further down the river. "I'll bet I could have hit it."

They all turned as a shout sounded from somewhere in the distance. "What was that?" asked Sam.

"Sounded like voices," said Caitlin.

"Was it from down here or up on the bridge?" Sam craned his neck to see up above them, but the angle made it impossible to see who might be up there.

"I think it was upriver." Derek leaped from his rock. "I'll go check it out. Maybe somebody will let me join their fishing party."

"What about Sam's glasses?" asked Caitlin.

"We can look for those along the way," said Derek, already starting up the thin trail of bent grass that followed the water.

Sam pointed in the other direction. "I think they would have landed back there."

"Fine. You two stay here," Derek called over his shoulder. "I'm going to go investigate."

"I hope he gets eaten by a bear," Sam muttered as his brother ran off. He stared above them and tried to move beneath where they'd been standing on the bridge.

"You think they'd have come this far?" asked Caitlin, following behind him.

Sam poked at the grass with his shoe half-heartedly. "Not really. I told you it was hopeless. Even if we find them, they're probably broken. My mom's going to kill me."

Caitlin pushed back a clump of ferns and searched through the wispy leaves. "She'll understand. You didn't mean to. Besides, she knows what it's like having Derek around. I don't think she'll be too shocked."

Sam chuckled. "Yeah, I guess."

Caitlin stood and peered upriver. "What's he doing over there?"

Sam turned and saw Derek crouched in the high grass just before a bend in the river. It looked like he was watching something. "There's no telling."

"Come on," said Caitlin. "Let's go see. Just watch where you step in case we happen upon your glasses."

Derek waved a warning as they approached, so they both sank lower and huddled behind him.

"What are you looking at?" Sam hissed.

Derek pointed to a spot further up the river, next to an old stone bridge support that rose to one of the original railroad trestles. "Over there."

Some boys were swimming in the river at the base of the support. A few more were standing on the rocks with their shirts off. It was a mixture of white and Black kids, probably six or seven altogether. Sam couldn't tell for sure with his glasses off, but they looked like teenagers, most likely a little older than Derek.

A flash of movement on the trestle caught his eye about twenty feet above the water. "There's somebody up there."

"Yeah," said Derek. "That's who I was watching."

"What's that in his hand?" asked Caitlin. "What's he doing?"

It was too far away for Sam to make out the details, but the boy appeared to be leaning back from the stones and working on something up near his head.

"I think he's tagging the stones," said Derek.

"Tagging?" asked Sam.

"You know, graffiti art. Can't you see the red spray paint?"

"They're defacing the bridge?" Caitlin moved like she was about to march over and yell at them, but Derek grabbed her arm.

"Stay here. It's not our business."

Caitlin shook her head. "But I told you, that bridge is from the Civil War. It's part of history."

"You might be part of history if you go over there," Derek whispered. "We don't know who those guys are."

Sam squinted harder. The kid on the trestle was white with a mop of red hair that was almost orange. "What's he painting? I can't tell from here."

Derek chuckled. "You should put on your glasses. Oh, wait, you dropped them—"

Sam slugged Derek in the arm but kept his eyes on the river.

"It's some kind of letters or design." Caitlin gave a long sigh. "I don't know why people think it's fun to make graffiti. It's just destructive, not to mention dangerous climbing up there."

While they'd watched the guy painting the stones, another boy had climbed out of the water and begun scaling the near side of the railroad trestle. "Tell me he's not gonna jump," Caitlin whispered.

Derek shifted lower in the grass. "Just stay down."

The second climber went even higher than the guy with the spray can, but then he stopped and reached for a rope attached to the trestle. He held the rope end in both hands, and then without hesitation pushed away from the stone, soaring through the air like a trapeze artist. At the height of his swing, he released the rope, flying into a tight flip before slipping smoothly into the water. All the rest of the boys whooped and hollered as the jumper swam to the shore and took a dramatic bow on the bank.

"Wow," said Derek. "That's cool. Maybe they'd let me try."

"That's crazy," muttered Sam. "Maybe we should leave."

Caitlin backed up. "Sam's right. We should get back to the bikes. If we're going to meet up with my dad for lunch, we need to keep going."

"Help you with something?" a voice called behind them.

They spun around to see another boy standing on the path with his hands on his hips. They'd been too focused on watching the swimmers to notice him approaching.

Derek spoke up first. "Oh, uh, sorry, we were just watching the acrobatics over there. My brother dropped his glasses over the bridge and we were trying to find them."

Sam looked at the kid in front of him. He was younger than the guys by the rope swing—probably about his own age. The boy's hair was cropped short against his dark skin and his Washington Wizards basketball jersey and shorts looked dry. He'd either just arrived, or hadn't been in the water with the others.

He stared at Sam. "Did you find them?"

"Huh?"

"Your glasses. Did you find them?"

"Oh," Sam answered. "No. I think they must have gone in the water."

"Ouch." The boy cringed and glanced at the fast-moving river.

Caitlin pointed up at the bridge. "We were just about to head up to our bikes on the trail."

"Hey, Jason, did you bring some friends with you?" someone behind them yelled out.

Sam glanced over his shoulder and saw that several of the older boys had climbed from the water and the trestle and were now walking toward them. This was going from bad to worse.

The boy with the orange hair started waving. He blew out a puff of smoke. "Who you talking to over there, Jason?"

"Think I could give that rope swing a try?" Derek pointed up at the stone trestle.

"Derek..." Sam muttered.

"I don't think you three should be down here," Jason said.

"Come on." Caitlin tugged on Sam's arm. "We're leaving." They both took several steps toward the woods.

"Not so fast," a deep voice ordered from the river. Sam turned to see a guy who was at least six feet tall. He had a mustache that made him look closer to eighteen. An eerie-looking spider tattoo covered his left shoulder. Sam considered whether they should make a run for it, but there was really nowhere to go except up the hill, and that wouldn't exactly make for a fast retreat.

Derek seemed to think similarly, because he motioned them back to the river. "How's it going, guys? That rope swing looks awesome."

"I love your rope swing," one of the other guys mocked in a high, goofy voice.

"What are you doing down here? Didn't my cuz tell you that tourists are supposed to stay up on the bridge? There's nothing but trouble down here."

"There's trolls under the bridge," someone growled.

The redheaded guy chuckled and stepped closer. "Or maybe they want to stay and swim with us."

Jason held up his hand. "Brennan, leave them alone, will you?" He turned to the big guy with the tattoo. "They were just leaving, DeShawn. They were looking for glasses that he dropped off the bridge."

"Well, they might have found more than they were lookin' for," DeShawn replied coolly. He strummed his fingers over his tattoo like he wanted to make sure everyone saw it.

"So, you like our swing, do ya, kid?" one of the guys said. "Wanna try it?"

Sam shook his head, trying to stop Derek before he did anything else stupid, but he was too late. "I, uh… sure, why not? It looks fun."

DeShawn seemed to be the leader of the group, and was also apparently Jason's cousin. He peered down at them like he was in deep concentration. It gave Sam the creeps.

"What do you think, DeShawn?" asked another of the guys. "Should we let him ride the fun swing?" Everyone in their group cracked up again with laughter.

DeShawn glanced upward and shook his head. "Nah, I don't think so."

Sam exhaled, relaxing a bit. Thank goodness. Now they could just get back up on the bridge.

"I think this one should do it." He grabbed Sam's arm, a sinister grin spreading across his face.

CHAPTER SEVEN

What did DeShawn just say? That Sam was going to have to go on the rope swing? Maybe he'd misheard. Maybe DeShawn meant Jason.

"What? No way," shouted Derek. "We're leaving."

Caitlin reached out and grabbed Sam's hand. "You can't make him do that. He's scared of heights!"

Sam closed his eyes as the group roared with laughter. That was probably the worst thing that she could have said.

"Sam, Caitlin, come on." Derek took a step toward the hill, but two of the guys ran over and blocked the path.

"Where do you think you're going?" they cackled.

"Oh, he's so scared," said Brennan, the red-haired guy. He grabbed Caitlin's arm. "Maybe your girlfriend isn't quite so chicken."

"Stop it!" screamed Caitlin. "Let go of me, you jerk!"

"Okay, I'll do it!" Sam suddenly shouted.

Everyone stopped and turned toward him.

"Well, all right," said DeShawn. "Maybe the little guy's got some backbone after all." He nodded at Brennan, who frowned but dropped Caitlin's arm.

"Sam, don't do it," she said, stepping closer.

"DeShawn, just let them go, man." Jason seemed like he was trying to help, but he clearly didn't hold much sway in the group.

DeShawn smiled. "Sure, no problem, cuz. Right after he goes off the swing." He turned back to Sam. "It's just water, kid. Not like you're jumping onto concrete or anything."

"As long as he misses that rock," said Brennan. "That's as good as concrete."

"Oh yeah," said another guy. "Remember the time Antione hit his foot? Doctor said it broke in two places."

Sam felt a bead of sweat drip down his forehead.

"I told you," said Derek. "I'll go. Let him be."

"Sit down and shut up." DeShawn pushed Derek to the dirt. "He said he'll do it, and now he's going to." He pointed to the stone trestle and gave Sam a shove. "Let's go. Jason can walk you out to the swing since he's so concerned about your safety."

Sam felt like he'd wandered into a bad dream as he walked along the riverbank. It was just water, right? What was the worst that could happen? It wasn't like he needed to do a fancy flip or anything.

He heard all the other guys trailing behind and laughing. "This should be good."

"Sam, be careful," called Caitlin.

When they reached the spot in the river where the guys had been swimming, Jason stripped off his shirt, shoes, and socks. He motioned for Sam to do the same. "The water's deep out there," he said softly. "It'll be fine. Just don't look down."

"Uh-huh," Sam answered, though he was hardly listening. As he waded into the river, the current was stronger than he expected. He lost his balance and splashed down, his hand hitting the gravel bottom.

"You do know how to swim, right, kid?" someone shouted.

Jason led him along a shallow section until they reached the old stone pillar. Sam looked up and realized the pillar didn't actually hold up the bridge. Newer, higher supports did that. It must have been an original section of the bridge from back when Lee's men were crossing during the war. "How am I supposed to climb this? There's no ladder."

Jason pointed up at the stones. "The edges jut out, almost like steps. Just grab a footing and work your way up." He pointed about twenty feet above them. "Do you see the rope?"

Sam squinted and made out a yellow rope tucked against the stone. "Yeah, I see it." He took a deep breath and tried to pretend it was just a ride at the water park. He grabbed at the rough stones and lifted a foot onto the ledge. He pushed himself up and then reached higher for another stone. Maybe Jason was right. If he didn't look down, it wouldn't be too bad.

His bare chest scraped against the jagged stones as Sam reached hand over hand, feeling his way up. It seemed like he wasn't making any progress at all, but then he saw the spot where Brennan had been spray-painting.

"You're almost there," Jason called from below a little later. "Reach up. You can probably touch the rope."

Sam raised his left hand slowly, still clutching the rock as hard as he could with his right. His wet, bare feet were aching from the rough stones. His fingertips brushed against the nylon rope. He reached and strained for it again and this time clutched it securely. But now what?

He suddenly realized climbing up had been the easy part. He slowly pivoted his head out toward the water. Derek and Caitlin were standing with the guys on the riverbank. He couldn't make out their expressions, but he saw Caitlin wave.

He should have just grabbed the rope and jumped, but he didn't. Instead, he did what Jason had told him not to do. He looked down at the water. That was a mistake, because as soon as he did, his stomach felt like it was already in a midair flip. The reason he hated heights was because they always made him dizzy.

Sam squeezed the rock in a tight bear hug, suddenly petrified to let go. He was only twenty feet in the air, but it felt like he was about to leap off the side of the 125-foot bridge above them. He remembered what Brennan had said about avoiding a rock. Where was that? He risked another look down. He had to. He didn't want to break his leg, or even worse, break his neck. He might be paralyzed for life. All because he dropped his stupid glasses.

Actually, that wasn't true. If Derek hadn't wandered over to where the group of boys was swimming, or better yet, never pushed Sam in the first place, they'd all be back up on the High Bridge Trail, riding straight toward Farmville. They might even be eating lunch with Mr. Murphy by now. This was exactly the kind of thing that he hated about his brother. He acted without thinking and got them into these kinds of—

A rock ricocheted off the trestle just above Sam's head. He flinched at the noise as tiny fragments of gravel rained down. His grip slipped a couple inches on the trestle, the rock scraping his stomach. What was that? He turned and recognized Brennan's red hair as he bent down and gathered stones on the riverbank.

"Are you crazy?" Sam shouted. He was throwing rocks at him!

"Dude, stop, you're going to hit him," yelled Jason.

Brennan just laughed. "Then he'd better jump, hadn't he?"

Sam watched wide-eyed as the kid held up a stone as big as a baseball. Brennan's arm pulled back, ready to launch.

It was now or never.

All at once, Sam released his bear hug on the stone. He pulled his right arm over to the rope, gripping it tight with both hands. He pushed off with his legs. At first, the line was slack, and he momentarily panicked that it wasn't actually attached to the trestle and he'd drop to his death into the shallows. But a split-second later, the rope tightened, and he was swinging in a slow arc out over the water.

But there was a problem. He didn't know when to let go.

He'd cleared the trestle, but now he'd started going up. He reached the top of the arc, freezing in midair, like time was standing still. Sam realized he'd missed his chance to let go like the other boy had, gracefully at the height of the pendulum swing, using its momentum for a smooth drop. But if he didn't release, he'd swing right back to where he'd started and smash against the trestle.

So he let go.

And then he was falling. Faster and faster, straight down to the water. He remembered that he still hadn't spotted the rock. He prayed he was heading toward the deep part of the river. He hit the surface awkwardly, butt-first and half on his back. Pain surged through his body as he plunged under, flailing to right himself when the current tumbled him about. He kicked and pulled his way back up to the surface, gasping for air. As his head broke through, Sam heard the hoots and jeers of the guys laughing on the riverbank.

"You all right?"

Sam wiped the water from his eyes and saw Jason reaching toward him to pull him back to the shallows. "Am I alive?" Sam sputtered, water spitting from his mouth.

"Yeah. You're not the most graceful flyer in the world, but you're alive."

Sam waded to the shore and climbed up onto the dry ground where Derek and Caitlin were waiting. Derek handed him his clothes. "All I can say is… wow."

Sam pulled his shirt on. "Thanks."

"Did you hurt yourself?" asked Caitlin.

"No, I don't think so."

"You're a natural, kid," called DeShawn.

"Yeah, man, you sure you didn't use to be in the circus or something?" Another guy laughed, enjoying the free entertainment. "If he was, I think he was in the clown car."

"Hey, give him a break," said Derek. "He did what you wanted."

Brennan stepped right into Derek's face. "What did you say? There's still time for your girlie friend to have a go at finding that rock out there, you know. Maybe she won't be as lucky as your brother."

Caitlin tugged at Derek's arm. "Come on. We're leaving."

Sam finished pulling on his shoes and followed Caitlin and Derek up the trail. This time, the older boys didn't stop them, but Jason ran to catch up.

"Sorry about that. DeShawn likes to act tough and scare people. His buddies will go along with just about anything he says."

"I think you need a new group of friends," said Caitlin. "They're jerks."

"Yeah…" Jason looked down and kicked at the dirt. "But he's my cousin and all." He pointed to the other side of the bridge. "If you're going back up top, there's an easier way over there. Look for the trail right after the square rock with the paint on it."

"Okay, thanks," said Derek. He turned and started walking. "Come on, guys."

CHAPTER EIGHT

S am leaned over, his hands on his knees, and caught his breath at the top of the steep hill. They'd finally made it back to their bikes, but he hardly felt like continuing down the High Bridge Trail. His socks hadn't gone on straight over his wet feet. They rubbed at his skin, which was already sore from climbing on the stones. The scrapes on his stomach hurt, and his lower back still throbbed from the impact of the water.

He pulled his bike upright and walked it to the edge of the bridge. Even without his glasses he could see it was a long way down to the river. "You can't even see that stone trestle from here."

"They probably planned it that way so they'd be out of sight," said Caitlin, stopping next to him.

Sam shook his head, realizing how much worse things could have gone. Even so, this was more than he'd bargained for on their outing to Farmville.

"Sorry." Derek draped his arm over Sam's shoulder. "I never meant for you to have to do that."

Sam felt a twinge of anger building inside him, but he took a deep breath and pushed it away. He knew his brother was trying to be nice. It wasn't really Derek's fault. It was just one of those things. "It's okay."

"You smacked that water hard," said Derek. "Did it leave a mark?"

Sam pulled up his shirt and turned around.

"Ouch," said Caitlin. "It's red."

Sam looked at the red scrapes on his stomach from pressing against the trestle. He touched one with his finger and winced. "I wasn't sure when to let go."

Derek chuckled. "We noticed."

"How did it look?"

"Imagine an elephant trying to fly," said Derek.

Caitlin giggled. "It was pretty bad, to be honest."

Derek pointed to Sam's face. "Can you ride without your glasses?"

"Yes, I can ride. It's not like I'm blind. I got along perfectly well my whole life without them. I think I can ride my bike down the trail." He gave Derek an angry glare. "As long as people stay out of my way."

"Consider it done." Derek stepped back on his pedals. "Let's go. I'm hungry!"

Caitlin climbed onto her bike. "That's right. Dad said we can have lunch at a café on Main Street. He heard that their cheesesteaks are amazing."

"Really?" Sam's stomach growled. All that excitement had made him hungry.

"But let's not mention anything about what happened under the bridge, okay? I don't want him to worry, and there's really nothing he can do about it. I don't know if he'll even notice your glasses are missing."

"Works for me," replied Sam. He followed her up the trail, thinking about cheesesteaks.

* * *

SAM FELT like they'd been riding for days when the trail finally reached Farmville. His feet were really aching now, and his bike seat had turned to a cinder block miles ago. Mr. Murphy was waiting for them on the street. He waved as he saw them exit the trail and helped stow their bikes in the back of his truck before driving to lunch.

"Didn't I see you wearing glasses this morning, Sam?" Mr. Murphy asked after they'd ordered their food.

"Um… they were a little uncomfortable, so I took them off. I was afraid I'd lose them on the trail." He didn't like lying, but it was sort of true. He hadn't exactly taken them off, but they definitely came off.

"I'm starving," Derek exclaimed, quickly changing the subject.

"Biking a few miles will do that for you," said Mr. Murphy. "Are you still up for visiting the Moton Museum?"

"That's what we came for," said Caitlin.

Mr. Murphy had been right about the food—the cheesesteak was delicious. Almost as good as the one Sam'd had at Yankee Stadium with his dad before they'd moved south. Sam knew Philadelphia was supposed to have the best around, but he hadn't had a chance to try one of those yet.

"You know, I didn't pick this place for lunch just for the cheesesteaks," said Mr. Murphy.

"You didn't?" Sam said with his mouth full. A chunk of cheese dripped down his chin.

"Sam, use a napkin, will you?" said Derek.

Mr. Murphy chuckled. "This building used to house Reid's Café, which was featured in the 1950s in a book called *The Negro Travelers' Green Book*."

"What was that for?" asked Caitlin.

"It was a guide that listed restaurants, hotels, and gas stations where African-Americans were welcome during Jim Crow. I believe Reid's was the only restaurant listed in Farmville."

Derek leaned back in his chair and stared out the window. "Is this the street where the student protests were?"

"It sure is," answered Mr. Murphy. "Main Street is the setting for many of the pictures from the *Freedom Now* project. Just up the road is the courthouse and First Baptist Church, where a lot of the meetings occurred during the protests. Martin Luther King even spoke there once."

"Can we try to find the exact spot from our picture?"

asked Derek. Sam and Caitlin had updated him on everything they'd learned from Natalie and shown him the picture they had chosen to start with.

"I don't see why not." Mr. Murphy grinned at Sam still chomping on his sandwich. "If we can pull Sam away from that cheesesteak, that is."

Sam frowned but kept eating. "What? It's good!"

Once Sam had finished, they walked out onto the sidewalk as Mr. Murphy paid the check at the counter. Sam shielded his eyes from the sun and looked up and down the street. He saw the red brick church Mr. Murphy had mentioned and another official-looking building across the street. "Is that the police station where the pictures were stored?"

"I believe it is." Mr. Murphy nodded as he joined them on the street. "And up there is where the shopping center and the movie theater used to be. I think that's where your picture was taken."

They walked over and stood on the sidewalk in front of where the storefront had been. Sam tried to imagine holding a sign and protesting against the injustice of the school closings with all kinds of people staring at him. It would have taken a lot of bravery and determination for sure.

"It seems like just an ordinary street," Sam said.

"That's why it's important to dig deeper," said Caitlin. She waved down the street. "If we didn't study history, we wouldn't know that something really important happened here."

"I guess that's why we're going to the museum," said Sam as they walked back to the truck. They drove up the road past the campus of Longwood University and stopped at a red brick building. Sam read the sign out front. "Robert Russa Moton Museum."

"Kinda small for a museum," said Derek, as they pulled into the parking lot.

"Would you rather it be bigger so we could spend the whole day?" asked Sam.

"Good point," said Derek. "This will be fine."

"It used to be the school for Black students here in Farmville," said Mr. Murphy as he lifted their bikes from the truck bed.

"Kinda small for a school too," added Derek.

"I think that's part of the point," said Sam. "Right?"

Mr. Murphy nodded. "I think so. But I'd bet you'll learn more inside. I'll be meeting with someone back at Longwood while you look around. There's a bike rack. You're okay riding over to the campus to meet me when you're done here?"

"We'll be fine, Daddy," said Caitlin, securing her bike and then waving goodbye. "Come on, guys. Let's go in!"

Past the entrance steps was a small gift shop. A woman stood behind the visitors' desk. "Greetings! Welcome to the Moton Museum."

"Thanks!" said Derek. "We're here to do some investigating."

The woman raised her eyebrows. "Investigating?"

"Actually," said Caitlin, "we'd like to take the tour

first, but afterward we're scheduled to speak with someone named Tiffany."

Derek groaned softly. "The tour? Really? Can't we just, you know, roam around?"

Caitlin elbowed him in the ribs. "Hush. This is an important place."

The woman smiled. "Of course. I'll let Ms. Williams know you're here." She spoke briefly into a telephone receiver and then turned back to their group. "Why don't you follow me?" She led them up the hall to a small auditorium with a wooden gym floor. A curtained stage was at the far end, and signs, quotations, and pictures filled the walls.

"Well, hello!" A youngish Black woman with a cheery face walked around the corner toward them. "I'm Tiffany Williams, and I'll bet two of you are Caitlin and Sam…"

"They are. And I'm Derek." He reached out and shook her hand heartily. "I'm kind of the brains of the operation here."

"Give me a break," moaned Sam.

"Is that right?" Tiffany laughed and motioned them to a row of seats in the middle of the auditorium. "Well, either way, Natalie Roberts tells me you're helping her with her *Freedom Now* project."

"That's right," replied Caitlin. "She has some new mystery photos that were discovered from the 1963 protests. We're trying to identify some of the students." She pulled an envelope from her backpack and held up the picture that they'd chosen to research first. "This girl, specifically."

Tiffany took the picture and eyed it carefully. "Mmm," she breathed. "Such courage those kids showed. They didn't know what a significant trail they were blazing for the entire country."

"You don't happen to recognize her, do you?" asked Derek. "That would make our jobs a lot easier."

Tiffany shook her head. "Afraid I don't, but the museum has some strong connections with folks in the community who might be able to help. As you can imagine, many of the students from the protests have moved or passed away at this point, but we still have quite a few who live right here in the Farmville area."

"You think they might help us?" asked Sam. Tracking down the girl in the picture sounded fun, but it had also seemed like a long shot after so much time.

Tiffany smiled. "I'll tell you what. Why don't you three watch the short video we have here in the auditorium? It recreates the 1951 school assembly where Barbara Johns rallied her fellow students to begin the protest. I'll make a couple phone calls to some folks I think could help." She raised the picture. "May I hold on to this for a few minutes?"

"Sure," answered Caitlin.

"Can I ask a question?" said Derek. "What kind of name is Moton for a museum, anyway? Isn't that some kind of music?"

Sam shook his head. "That's Motown, stupid."

61

Tiffany laughed. "That's a very understandable question, Derek. You're probably thinking of the African-American record label from Detroit. That's an interesting, but entirely different story."

"Moton was the name of this school, wasn't it?" asked Caitlin.

"That's right." Tiffany waved her arm at the room. "This was once the high school for Prince Edward County's Black students. It's named after Robert Russa Moton, a local educator in the early 1900s. He went on to take over as principal of the Tuskegee Institute, an important, historically Black college founded by Booker T. Washington, one of the most prominent Black leaders around the turn of the twentieth century."

"Tuskegee," said Sam, thinking about the odd-sounding word. "Where have I heard that name before?"

"Well, the Tuskegee Airmen were the first African-American flyers in the US military during World War II," said Tiffany.

"Oh, yeah." Sam turned to Derek. "Remember, we saw a movie about them."

Tiffany nodded. "They faced a lot of discrimination in and out of the military. Keep in mind, many of the places they came from were still subject to the segregationist laws of the Jim Crow South."

"Why do they call it that?" Sam knew from talking with Mr. Haskins that it meant Black people weren't allowed to use the same facilities as white people, but he didn't know why.

"The name came from an old song and dance routine in the 1800s, but it became a slang term for Black people. When the former Confederate states began passing segregationist laws after the Civil War and Reconstruction, they became referred to as Jim Crow laws because of the people they applied to."

"That's still a strange name."

"I agree," said Tiffany, "but don't let the name lessen their significance. Sadly, Jim Crow laws enforced racial segregation in the South well into the 1960s. You may have learned about a historic Supreme Court case from 1896 called *Plessy vs. Ferguson.*"

"That was about 'separate but equal,' right?" said Caitlin.

Tiffany nodded. "Very good. Except in practice, things remained very much separate, but not usually equal. Conditions of the facilities for African-Americans were often greatly inferior to those designated for whites."

"And the Supreme Court said that was okay?" asked Sam.

"For a long time, leaders in the South did nothing about it. Let's just put it that way," said Tiffany. "Which leads us to what happened right here. Since public education in the South was segregated, Black students were prohibited from attending the same schools as white students. And many of the Black schools like this one were falling apart. This building had very poor heating in the winter, and many of the small outbuildings scattered around the property were little more than tar paper shacks. They better resembled chicken houses than classrooms. Students had to sit near woodstoves, sometimes even holding umbrellas above their heads to stay out of the rain that leaked through the roof. And the school held more than twice the number of students they designed the building for."

Sam looked at the picture of a teenage girl on the back wall. "So, what did Barbara Johns do, exactly?"

Tiffany's face lit up at her name. "Barbara was an astounding young woman. Though she was just sixteen, she was tired of the substandard conditions of her school. One morning she missed her bus, and while she waited for a car to come by that might bring her into the town —she lived fifteen miles out in the country, mind you— the school bus for the white school blew right past her, and it was only half-filled."

"It didn't pick her up?" asked Sam.

Tiffany shook her head. "They wouldn't do that in those days."

"That would have made me mad," fumed Caitlin.

"Yes, and that may have been Barbara's breaking point, too, because soon afterward, she decided to do something about it. On April 23, 1951, Barbara organized a group of students to put together a strike. When the principal was out of the building, they called all the students into this auditorium, and the football team escorted all the teachers from the room."

"We should do that at our school," said Derek, a

mischievous grin on his face. "Who wants teachers around, anyway?"

"It might sound fun, but in this case, they did it so the teachers wouldn't get in trouble," Tiffany explained. "Barbara knew that if teachers, or even their parents, were involved in the protest, as adults they could face serious consequences like losing their jobs or other discrimination. So Barbara convinced the students here at Moton High School to march out of the building together in protest of their school's poor conditions."

"Weren't they afraid they'd be arrested," asked Sam, "even if they were kids?"

"Barbara assured her classmates that 'the Farmville jail isn't big enough to hold us,' and I guess she was right." Tiffany stood and pointed to a curtained stage on the far side of the auditorium. "Which is what this short video is all about. It's a recreation of the assembly that occurred on this very stage when Barbara organized the student strike."

"Cool," said Derek. "Maybe I'll organize a student strike at our school."

"Theirs was for a good reason, Derek," said Caitlin. "They were protesting unfair conditions."

"Trust me, if you were in Mrs. Franklin's English class last year, you'd know about unfair conditions. She gave us homework three days—"

Sam kicked his brother's shin. "Stop, this isn't the same and you know it."

Derek seemed to notice that Tiffany was giving him a

disapproving look too. And surprisingly, he shut his mouth.

"Sorry," said Caitlin. "He's a little self-indulgent."

Derek glared at her. "I'm not sure what that means, but I don't appreciate it."

Tiffany laughed. "I'm glad you're here. A big part of why we have this museum is to remember the struggle and sacrifice made by people like Barbara. While your life may not include the same challenges, understanding the struggles of others helps us be more empathetic."

Sam sighed. His brother could be an idiot. But what Tiffany said was true. While he sometimes wished he didn't have to go to school, he couldn't imagine having to attend class in a building where the roof was leaking and the walls were falling down. It was easy to take what they had for granted. "Thanks for explaining things," he said.

Tiffany smiled. "It's my pleasure." She held up the photo. "And thank you all for your interest in helping identify this young friend. Maybe we'll get lucky and I'll find someone who recognizes her." She walked to the wall next to the stage and lowered the lights. "I'll see you in a few minutes."

CHAPTER NINE

T he curtain on the auditorium stage opened to reveal a screen. The video wasn't one of those normal documentaries they watched in class, which were more like news reports. This was a reenactment, like the one they'd seen live at St. John's Church of Patrick Henry's "give me liberty or give me death" speech. The video had been filmed in this auditorium, with teenage actors portraying the students from back in 1951. An actress playing Barbara Johns stood at a podium with several other classmates and spoke about the need to protest the conditions of their school.

Sam couldn't imagine getting up on stage and talking to his entire school about anything, let alone leading a student strike. Derek would have the nerve but probably not the conviction needed to take charge of something that important. Sam glanced at Caitlin and thought that she probably could do it. It sounded like Caitlin and Barbara Johns might have a lot in common.

When the video finished, the lights gradually rose, and Tiffany walked back into the auditorium with another African-American woman. The new lady was elderly, but seemed spry as she smiled in their direction.

"That was amazing," said Caitlin. "I felt like Barbara was right here rallying us to join the protest."

"That's the idea," said Tiffany. "I'm glad you enjoyed it. Kids, I'd like to introduce you to Mrs. Eloise Baines. She played a very important role in what you just saw up on the screen. She was one of the students who walked out of this room with Barbara Johns back in 1951."

"Wow." Caitlin reached out and shook Mrs. Baines' hand. "It's an honor to meet you."

Mrs. Baines smiled. "Nice to meet you, children. It's wonderful to see young people interested in history. Particularly in civil rights."

"Did you really know Barbara Johns?" asked Derek.

Mrs. Baines nodded. "I most certainly did. She was a few years older than me in school, the same year as my older brother, Kenneth."

"Is that really what it was like?" Sam pointed to the screen. "The assembly where she organized the strike?"

"It surely was," Mrs. Baines answered. "Interestingly, most people thought of Barbara as quiet and shy before she led the protest. Even her younger sister was shocked when she saw her up on the stage. But Barbara was determined. She seemed driven by a divine force to fight for change. She was willing to be a voice and stand up for what was right when many folks much older than her hadn't done so."

"She must have become a real celebrity," said Derek, staring at her picture on the back wall. "Today she'd have like a million followers on social media. Maybe even her own podcast."

"I'm afraid that's not exactly how things worked out," Tiffany answered. "The strike lasted for two weeks. During that time, Barbara, other student leaders, and Reverend Griffin from the First Baptist Church petitioned help from two courageous lawyers from the NAACP named Oliver Hill and Spottswood Robinson. They filed a lawsuit in federal court that pushed for desegregated schools."

"Sweet," said Sam. "I guess the strike worked then."

Mrs. Baines shook her head. "Yes, and no. They lost that court case, but next they appealed to the US Supreme Court, and theirs became one of five cases that merged into the famous *Brown vs. Board of Education* in 1954."

"My dad told us about that one," said Caitlin. "It ruled that segregation in public schools was unconstitutional, right?"

"Okay, so it took a little longer," said Derek. "But I'll bet Barbara was famous after that."

"I wish it would have been that simple," said Tiffany. "After the student strike, Barbara and her family faced increasing persecution, including at least one threat on

STEVEN K. SMITH

her life. Her parents worried for her safety and sent her off to Alabama to live with her uncle, Vernon Johns. He was a prominent civil rights leader. Vernon was the fiery minister at the Dexter Avenue Baptist Church in Montgomery, Alabama, and was later succeeded by another famous leader you might have heard of—a young Dr. Martin Luther King, Jr."

"Wow," said Sam. "It's like they're connected."

Mrs. Baines smiled. "Could be, young man. Sometimes I think God had a special plan for Barbara Johns."

"Does she still live in Alabama," asked Derek, "or did she move back to Virginia after things settled down?"

"Well, things didn't exactly settle down," explained Tiffany. "After the *Brown* decision a few years later, while the Johns family was out of town, someone burned their house down."

"Oh my gosh," said Caitlin. "Why would anyone do that? She was just trying to stand up for what was right."

Mrs. Baines nodded. "But that doesn't mean folks are going to like it. Sometimes change comes slow."

"What happened to Barbara?" asked Sam.

"Barbara kept a fairly low profile. She went to college, married a minister, raised five children, and worked as a librarian in Philadelphia."

"I'd love to meet her," said Caitlin.

Mrs. Baines pursed her lips. "Several of her relatives are still living, but Barbara died of cancer in 1991 at the age of only fifty-six."

"Oh, that's so sad," said Caitlin.

"Yes, but she did an amazing thing," said Mrs. Baines. "And it inspired many people to follow in the path she helped establish."

"Including the protests ten years later that were captured in the pictures you all are investigating," added Tiffany.

"Hang on." Derek crossed his arms with a confused look on his face. "How could the strike in the pictures be ten years after what Barbara did at her school? You said the Supreme Court ruled it was illegal for schools to be separate, to be segregated, I mean."

Tiffany nodded. "Yes, they declared it unconstitutional, but sometimes setting a law and having it enforced are two different things. Barbara's student strike lasted two weeks, but even after the *Brown* ruling three years later, things didn't change right away. In fact, ten long years later, the courts were still pushing Virginia to finally desegregate. That's when the county leaders here in Prince Edward decided it was better to close down the schools than to allow students of different races to attend together."

Caitlin shook her head. "I can't even believe that."

Sam's brain was spinning with all the information. He'd thought Barbara Johns' protest had stopped the racial discrimination, but things seemed a lot more complicated than that. He noticed that Mrs. Baines was holding the old photo. "So how about our picture? Do you recognize the girl?"

Mrs. Baines smiled, but she didn't answer right away.

She had a faraway look in her eyes. "It's funny, even though all of that happened almost sixty years ago, the memories come flooding back to my mind like it was yesterday. And these, these were some brave kids. I've seen some of the photos from this protest before, but not this one."

"So I guess you didn't know her?" asked Derek.

Mrs. Baines shook her head. "I'm afraid I can't tell you her name."

"Keep in mind that Mrs. Baines was in high school during Barbara Johns' time," said Tiffany. "The protests in this picture were nearly ten years later."

"I was a grown woman by then," said Mrs. Baines. "I'd met Hank—that's my husband—a couple years after high school. We married and moved just outside of Lynchburg shortly thereafter."

"That's okay." Caitlin looked down in disappointment. "I'm sure we'll figure it out."

"But I'll bet Marlene would know," said Mrs. Baines.

Caitlin glanced back up. "Marlene?"

"That's my sister. She's five years younger than me. She missed her senior year of high school when the schools were closed, but she finished up at Kittrell Junior College across the border in North Carolina. That's where a number of students were sent. For many of them, like Marlene, it was the first time they'd ever been away from home."

"Wow," said Caitlin. "I can't imagine having to do that either."

"Can we show your sister the picture?" asked Sam.

"Certainly," said Mrs. Baines. "I'm sure she'd be happy to help. But it might take a couple weeks. Do you mind waiting, or is it a rush?"

"It's not exactly a rush, but—" started Caitlin.

"A couple weeks?" asked Derek. "Is she away on vacation or something?"

Mrs. Baines shook her head. "She lives in Atlanta, but I can send it to her in the mail. She loves receiving letters."

"Um…" Sam tried not to sound rude. But like their neighbor, Mr. Haskins, he knew that some older people didn't always think about using technology. "Why don't we just take a picture of it and you can text her?"

Mrs. Baines stared at them for a couple moments like the wheels were turning in her head. Then her arm shot forward and slapped Sam's knee. He yelped in surprise and everyone burst out laughing.

"I always forget about how technology has changed so much." Mrs. Baines patted his knee tenderly. "I'm sorry, dear. I didn't hurt you, did I?"

For an old lady, she packed a punch. "Um, no. That's okay."

"Do you have a smartphone, Mrs. Baines?" asked Caitlin.

"I sure do. Used it just last week, as a matter of fact!" The old woman rummaged through her oversized purse, emptying what seemed like nearly half the contents of her house out onto the table before she held up a shiny new iPhone.

Derek's eyebrows rose. "That's the new model I've been asking Mom and Dad for. How'd you get that?"

Mrs. Baines laughed. "My grandson bought it for me. He said it would help me keep in touch, but I haven't used it much." She leaned closer to them. "He's a very successful lawyer up in Northern Virginia."

Derek eyed her with a new sense of admiration. "Wow, you're full of surprises, Mrs. B."

"Why don't I help Mrs. Baines contact her sister," said Tiffany. "In the meantime, you three can walk through the rest of the exhibits. There's a lot of information that might interest you, not just about Barbara Johns, but also about the school closings, Massive Resistance, and important court cases. Some key parts of our country's civil rights movement emerged from right here in tiny Farmville."

CHAPTER TEN

While Mrs. Baines and Tiffany worked to connect with Marlene, Sam, Caitlin, and Derek walked through several small rooms of exhibits. Sam didn't remember learning about much of this in social studies, but he figured maybe there would be more about it all in high school.

He studied a picture of Robert Kennedy, who he thought was President Kennedy's brother. Beneath it was a quotation from a speech he'd given that said "the only places on earth not to provide free public education are Communist China, North Vietnam, Sarawak, Singapore, British Honduras—and Prince Edward County, Virginia."

"I don't know where Sarawak is, but that doesn't seem like a good list to be on," said Caitlin, reading over his shoulder. They walked along the wall, staring at the different displays from various periods of the civil rights movement.

Caitlin pointed at the glass. "Look at this one—it says that a woman named Irene Morgan refused to give up her seat on the bus for white passengers here in Virginia in 1944. That was nine years before Rosa Parks did a similar thing in Alabama. And listen to this—even though the Supreme Court said it was unconstitutional to have racial segregation on buses, Virginia didn't enforce any changes for decades."

"I think what your dad said is right," said Sam.

"What's that?"

"Virginia doesn't have a great record for doing the right thing on these kinds of issues."

He called Derek over to the next display that caught his attention. "Hey, remember Dorothy Vaughan from that movie we watched, *Hidden Figures*?"

Derek nodded. "Yeah, that was a good movie. Wasn't she one of those women who were math whizzes for NASA?"

"Exactly," answered Sam. "But it says that before she worked at NASA, she was a teacher right here at Moton High School."

"Wow," said Caitlin. "That's incredible." She waved Sam over to the wall display she was reading. "There's President Lyndon Johnson signing the *Civil Rights Act of 1964* and then the *Voting Rights Act of 1965*. Do you recognize the man behind him in both pictures?"

Sam stared closer. "Is that Martin Luther King?"

"I think so."

"Look at this section," called Derek. "They've titled it Massive Resistance. That sounds big."

Sam stepped next to Derek and looked up at a picture labeled "Senator Harry F. Byrd." "But not in a good way, I don't think."

Caitlin started reading the quote next to the picture.

"'If we can organize the Southern states for massive resistance to this order I think that, in time, the rest of the country will realize that racial integration is not going to be accepted in the South.' Senator Harry Flood Byrd, 1954."

"See what I mean about Virginia," said Sam. "Not good."

Caitlin shook her head. "That was two years before the schools were closed in Prince Edward County. Imagine what it would feel like to have the state leaders trying to block what the Supreme Court already said should happen. It's crazy."

"Even I don't work that hard to keep Sam from doing things," said Derek, as they reached the end of the exhibit. "Hey, here come Tiffany and Mrs. Baines."

Caitlin waved as they all met at the edge of the auditorium. "Did you find anything out?"

Tiffany smiled as she held up the picture and a Post-It note. "We have a name!"

"Of the girl in the picture?" asked Sam.

"That's right." Mrs. Baines grinned. "I thought Marlene would remember something. She knew just about all the folks in town. She dug out one of her old yearbooks and found the name under the girl's picture. She can likely help with other photos too if you need it."

Tiffany handed over the Post-It. "Miriam Cartwright," Caitlin read aloud.

"That's her name?" asked Sam. "The girl in the photo?"

"We believe so," said Tiffany.

"According to the yearbook, she was a grade behind my sister in school. Marlene thinks Miriam might still have relatives here in Farmville. The county records office should have a last known address or contact information. Who knows, she might still live here."

"Sweet!" Sam felt the excitement returning to their mission. Maybe it wasn't a wild goose chase.

"Well, I guess that's where we're going next," said Caitlin. "Can we ride our bikes there?"

Tiffany nodded. "I don't see why not, if you're careful. It's just up the road on Main Street, next to the county courthouse."

Derek rolled his eyes. "Great. I've been itching to get to the county records office for a while."

Sam elbowed him to be quiet before turning back to Mrs. Baines. "Thanks for your help."

Mrs. Baines nodded. "It's my pleasure. Frankly, it's a joy to see young people interested in learning more about those times. Despite many gains over the years, the struggle continues, I'm afraid. And the more people contributing, the better."

Tiffany called ahead and told the man at the county records office what they needed. They rode their bikes up the street, and just a few minutes after finding the right building, a man appeared behind the records counter. "Afraid we don't have any listing for Miriam Cartwright."

"You don't?" Caitlin's shoulders sunk. "How can that be?"

"We know she went to high school here," said Derek.

The man peered out at them over his dusty glasses. "However, as I was about to say, there is a listing for a Miriam Cartwright Foster."

"Could that be her married name?" asked Caitlin.

"Maybe," said Sam. He looked back at the man. "Do you have any information for that name?"

"You're in luck." The man held out a yellowed index card. "We have a last known address."

"Is it close by?" asked Caitlin.

"Well, she doesn't live here in the building, if that's what ya mean." The man cackled at his own lame joke like it was the funniest thing ever said. "But the address is just on the edge of town."

"Do you have an email address or a phone number?" asked Derek. "Or a social media account? That would be even better."

"Afraid not, young man. What we have is what we

STEVEN K. SMITH

have. You're lucky there was even an address. But I'll let you in on a little secret…" Derek's eyes lit up as the old man leaned forward across the counter.

"They didn't have internet back then," the man whispered, then he straightened up and broke into another wild cackle.

Sam frowned. "Okay, well, thanks, sir."

"I think that guy's putting a little too much sugar in his coffee," Derek muttered as Caitlin pulled out her phone to look up the address.

"Maybe, but he's right about the address." She held up a map on her phone. "Look, it's only a few blocks away. We can ride over there now!"

Sam stopped walking. "Wait—now?" He glanced at the clock on the wall. It was almost three.

Caitlin nodded. "Sure, why not? We're already here in town. Isn't this what we came for? To find the girl in the picture? My dad has plenty to keep him busy over on campus. I'll just let him know we need more time."

"Yeah…" Sam answered, "but we found out her name. Miriam Cartwright Foster. Why do we have to knock on her door?"

"Oh, come on, Sam, don't get squeamish now," Derek chided. "You don't even have to say anything. I'll do all the talking."

Sam rolled his eyes. "Oh, that makes me feel much better." He tried to think about why he felt uncomfortable walking up to a stranger's house as they returned to their bikes. Maybe it was because of what had happened under the bridge. He didn't feel like barging in on anyone else unexpectedly. Not that anyone else was likely to make him jump off a rope swing, but his nerves were frayed. He'd had enough conversation with strangers for one day.

His mom had told him that some people are extroverts and others are introverts. He didn't like being called an introvert—that made it sound as if he didn't want to talk to people, which wasn't true. And he hated it when people called him quiet. Just because he wasn't obnoxious like Derek didn't mean he wanted to sit alone in a dark room and stare at the wall.

Mom said that wasn't exactly what it meant, but that it was more about what charged your batteries versus drained them. She said some people go to a party and feel more energized, while others feel exhausted after a lot of socializing. That made a little more sense to him. He liked to hang out with people, but sometimes it did kind of wear him out. Like today.

Sam remembered what Tiffany had said about Barbara Johns—that folks thought of her as shy. He wondered if she had hated that label too. He supposed her story was a good reminder that people can push themselves outside their regular comfort zone if they really want to. Barbara did, and her actions changed things forever. Sam may have been forced to jump off the rope swing into the river, but no one was about to burn his house down or force him to go to school out of the state. He took a deep breath. Maybe knocking on someone's door wasn't such a big thing.

Caitlin followed her phone's directions, turning onto a tree-lined street with sidewalks along the road. There were rows of well-kept split-level style houses. She slowed halfway down the block, glancing at the map.

"328. This is it!" She stopped and leaned her bike against a tree by the walkway that led to the front porch.

"Hang on," called Sam. "What are we going to do, just march up and ask if Miriam Cartwright lives here?"

"Basically," said Caitlin.

"But this might be an old address. She could have moved out thirty years ago."

"Well, there's only one way to find out, Sam." Derek strode past them up to the porch. He rang the doorbell and grinned back at them. "See? It's easy."

"Come on." Caitlin followed up the walk just as the door opened. A little girl stood behind the screen door. She was probably about kindergarten-age, and her dark hair was formed into a series of tight braids that fell down both sides of her face. The image of a unicorn jumping over a rainbow filled her T-shirt.

She stared out at them suspiciously from the other side of the screen. "May I help you?"

"Let me guess," said Derek. "You're not Miriam."

"Miriam?" repeated the girl. "Who's that?"

Caitlin pushed Derek back and leaned down to the girl's eye level. "Hi there. We're looking for Ms. Miriam Cartwright. Does she live here?"

The girl didn't answer. She just turned back inside the house and yelled at the top of her lungs, "Mommy! Some *weird* kids are here." She said the word *weird* as if they'd just arrived from another planet. Which, if she'd known them, wouldn't have seemed all that unusual, since Derek did act like he was from another planet most of the time.

Sam began to squirm on the porch step. He wondered what he'd do if three kids showed up at his door and asked for his grandma. It *was* kind of weird.

"There's what?" a woman's voice answered from further inside the house. "Angie, is someone at the front door?"

The little girl ran out of sight toward where her mom's voice had come from. "They want to know if Maria's car is all right or something *weird* like that."

"Maria's car?" the woman answered. "What in the world? Okay, well let me go see what's happening. Haven't I told you not to answer the front door by yourself?"

"I know, Mommy, but the bell rang and you were busy painting. It would be *weird* if I didn't answer it."

They all held in a chuckle at the funny way the little girl kept using that word as they waited on the porch. A few moments later, the woman came into view. She was about Sam's mom's age, tall, and had her hair pulled back. Her oversized T-shirt was splattered with at least four different colors of paint. Sam wondered if she was an artist or just doing a little remodeling.

She looked surprised to see there were kids on the

porch. "Oh, I'm sorry, I couldn't quite make out what my daughter was saying. Didn't mean to leave you standing there."

The little girl, Angie, appeared at her mother's hip, staring out shyly from behind the edge of the painting T-shirt. "I told you it was something *weird.*"

The mom looked up with an exasperated expression. "Suddenly everything is *weird* with her."

Derek laughed and nodded at Sam. "I know exactly what you mean."

"Can I help you with something?" the mom asked. "We don't need any cookies."

"Hi." Caitlin smiled. "We're not selling anything. I'm Caitlin, and this is Sam and Derek. We're researchers from Richmond and the *Freedom Now* project at VCU."

The woman stared back like she wasn't registering what Caitlin was saying.

"Virginia Commonwealth University," said Derek.

She held up her hand. "I know what VCU is, honey. That's where I got my master's degree. But you all look a little young for college students. What are you research-ing? Did Angie say something about a car?" She took a half-step backward, like she was getting ready to close the door.

Sam sighed and decided he'd better do something before things turned even more awkward. "Do you know a Miriam Cartwright?"

A slight recognition flashed across the woman's face,

but she worked hard to hide it. "Why would you want to know that?"

Sam nudged Caitlin. "Show her the picture."

"Oh, right." Caitlin reached in and pulled the envelope from her bag. "We're working to track down the girl in this picture. It's from the student protests back in the summer of 1963. We were just at the Moton Museum, and we discovered that her name is Miriam Cartwright. The county records office showed that her married name might be Foster and listed this house as her last known address." Caitlin held up the square photo.

The woman stepped closer and stared through the screen. For a moment, Sam didn't think she'd recognized her, but then he heard her breath catch.

"Oh my," she said finally, breaking her stare to look back at them. Then she turned a latch and opened the screen door. "Please, come in."

"Why, Mommy?" asked Angie. "I don't see a car. Only bikes."

She ushered them through the foyer and into a living room and tossed several pillows off the couch. "Here, please, have a seat." She still held the picture, but her face had softened. "Where did you get this?"

"My dad is a photographer, and he's working with Mrs. Roberts at VCU on the *Freedom Now* project," explained Caitlin. "A whole batch of photos were found in the basement of the Farmville police station a few years ago, and the library is working to identify the protesters."

Angie leaned in to see. "Who's that in the picture, Mommy?'

"I'm getting the sense that you know her," said Derek. "Does she live here?"

The woman shook her head. "I'm afraid she's no longer with us. She passed away nearly five years ago." She stood and reached out her hand. "I'm sorry, I should have introduced myself. I'm Shanelle Thomas. Shanelle *Foster* Thomas. Cartwright was my mother's maiden name."

"Car ride?" Angie wriggled her nose at the picture. "This is your mommy? That's *weird*."

None of them could hold it in any longer and they all burst out laughing. "She's a riot." Caitlin leaned down. "How old are you?"

Angie pushed a wide handful of fingers at Caitlin's face. "I'm five."

Mrs. Thomas shook her head. "Four, sweetheart. You're four."

Angie looked insulted, but she turned back to the visitors on the couch. "I'm almost five," she whispered and then scooted around the furniture. "It's so *weird*!" she screamed as she bolted down the hall.

As she left, the sound of footsteps came from the porch and the screen door opened and slammed. "I'm home, Mom!" a boy's voice called. "I'm gonna take a shower."

"Just a moment, honey, come in here," Mrs. Thomas answered. "We have guests."

A boy bounded around the corner, basketball in hand. He stopped short at the sight of them sitting on the couch. His eyes opened wide.

Sam held his breath.

It was Jason. The kid from the river.

CHAPTER ELEVEN

"This is my son, Jason." Mrs. Thomas waved the boy over and rested her hand on his arm. The basketball slipped from under his arm and rolled across the floor. It was hard to tell who was more surprised—Jason seeing Sam, Derek, and Caitlin on his living-room couch, or the three of them seeing the boy from the river again.

"Jason, don't just stand there like a tree," said Mrs. Thomas. "Say hello."

He blinked his eyes and waved weakly. "Uh... hi." He looked like he'd rather be anywhere but there.

"How was basketball?" his mom asked. "Was the gym open?"

"What? I mean, uh, yeah, it was open. It was fun." He stared at them so intently, it felt like he was trying to bore holes right through them and into the couch. Sam figured it made sense considering what Jason and his mom had said about basketball.

Mrs. Thomas touched her son's arm and smiled. "He's working hard to make the eighth-grade team this year. They open up the gym over at the middle school sometimes on the weekend so he can work on his jump shot. Isn't that right, honey?"

Jason finally seemed to pull it together. "Yeah. Right, Mom." He reached down for his ball and nodded at the couch. "What are they doing here?"

Mrs. Thomas frowned. "Honey, they're right here. They can hear you. Don't be rude." She picked the photo up from the table. "Sam, Derek, and Caitlin—" She turned and looked at them quickly. "Do I have that right?"

Caitlin nodded. "Good memory."

"They're researching some old photos from the student protests right here in Farmville in the '60s. It turns out the girl in this photo is my mother."

Jason scrunched his eyebrows and took the picture from her hand. "That's Granny Foster? For real?"

Mrs. Thomas nodded. "That's right. Back when she was in high school. You were probably too young to remember her talking about it before she passed, but it was always one of her proudest moments. She was just a couple years older than you are now at the time this picture was taken. Don't you remember me telling you how she was part of the civil rights movement?"

"Kinda."

"These kids…" Mrs. Thomas stopped herself and then looked at them. "I'm sorry, I didn't offer you anything to drink. Would you like some sweet tea?"

"Sure!" Derek answered enthusiastically before Sam could say no. They hadn't planned to spend all afternoon there. Little Angie had been cute, but now it felt awkward with Jason, like he didn't want them there.

Mrs. Thomas hopped up from her chair. "I'll be right back. Jason can keep you company in the meantime. I'll bet you all are nearly the same age."

Jason opened his mouth to object, but his mom was already in the kitchen. He frowned and dropped into the chair across from the couch and stared at them. "Please don't say anything to my mom about the river. I'm not supposed to be hanging out with those guys."

"Yeah," said Caitlin. "We kind of got that impression."

"Don't worry," said Derek. "We're cool." He reached out to bump fists, but Jason didn't raise his hand.

"Thanks." Jason leaned back and looked at Sam. "You okay? After…well, you know."

"His smackdown?" Derek laughed.

Sam shrugged. "I'll live."

"Sorry again about all that. I told you, DeShawn can get carried away. So…" He glanced to the kitchen and then back at the couch. "Where are you guys from? I haven't seen you around before today."

PICTURES AT THE PROTEST

"We live in Richmond," Caitlin answered.

"You a Wizards fan?" asked Derek.

"How'd you guess?"

"Well, your shirt…" Derek started, but then he realized it was a rhetorical question. "Oh."

"You play ball?"

Derek shrugged. "A little. We like the Knicks."

"Geez." Jason chuckled. "They stink."

"Yeah…"

"I like John Wall," said Caitlin. "He's your point guard, right?"

Sam raised his eyebrows. He'd never heard Caitlin talk about basketball before, although he thought Mr. Murphy watched sports sometimes. Maybe he liked the Wizards and Caitlin watched it with him.

"Yeah, he's great when he's not injured." Jason looked again to the kitchen, as if he was weighing whether it was better to have his mom in or out of the room. "So, you guys are what, in a research club for school or something?" He made it sound like the least interesting thing in the world.

Caitlin shook her head. "Actually, we just like solving mysteries. You know, tracking down clues that connect with history and finding lost treasures, that sort of thing."

"You may have read about us in the paper," added Derek, proudly rehashing one of his favorite lines. "They've featured us a few times."

"The newspaper?" asked Jason. "Nah, I don't think so. So, what, you're like those kids in *Scooby-Doo* that solve mysteries? Do you have a crime dog and stuff?"

Sam closed his eyes. This was terrible.

"No, it's not like that," Caitlin explained. "Sometimes we go looking for a lost artifact or treasure, and sometimes we just stumble across a mystery that needs to be solved. This time, my dad showed us a group of pictures like the one your grandma was in from the protests. We thought it would be fun to help identify the names of the kids in the pictures. It's like searching for a lost treasure too, in its own way."

"Huh," said Jason. "I guess that's kind of cool. I never really thought about my Granny like that. She died around the same time as my dad was deployed the first time—" He stopped himself and glanced at the kitchen. "So, I didn't know her much."

"Deployed?" asked Derek. "You mean like in the military?"

Jason nodded. "Yeah, he's back in Afghanistan."

"Wow," Derek said. "Does he get to drive a Humvee?"

"Sometimes, I guess."

Derek's eyes lit up. "That's cool."

Jason turned his basketball in his hands and looked at the wall. "What would be cool is if he was home."

Sam followed Jason's stare to a framed picture with a tall man in uniform surrounded by his smiling family. He didn't know how long Jason's dad had been gone from home, but that seemed really hard. Several oil paintings filled the next wall, each with bright colors in various abstract designs. Sam remembered seeing the paint on Mrs. Murphy's shirt. "Did your mom make all those?" he asked, trying to change the subject.

"Most of them," Jason answered. "She's kind of a part-time artist."

Mrs. Thomas walked back into the room with a tray of glasses. She set them on the coffee table and passed them one by one over to the kids on the couch. "I brought one for you too, honey, since you're chatting with us."

"Um, I'm not really chatting, Mom," Jason said, but she placed a hand on his leg to make it clear he wasn't leaving.

She turned back to the couch. "So, tell me more about what you're working on. The Freedom Project?"

"*Freedom Now*," said Caitlin. She described what Natalie had told them about the pictures and the goal to identify all the different students from the photos.

"That's such a great idea," said Mrs. Thomas. "It all happened before my time, obviously, but as a girl, my mother used to tell me stories about those years when the schools were closed. It was such a dark period for so many families here in Prince Edward County, but also in other parts of Virginia and throughout the South."

"Hold up," said Jason. "You mean the schools got closed back then, too?"

Derek grinned. "That's exactly what *I* said!"

Mrs. Thomas nodded. "They did, but not the way you're thinking. The only thing *wrong* with Granny Cartwright or anyone else who was going to that school was the color of her skin. At least in the view of the county leaders. After the *Brown* case said that educational segregation wasn't lawful, they refused to let their children integrate with ours. So instead, they just shut the whole system down and started their own private schools that their white children could attend. The ones with any money at least."

Jason raised his eyebrows. "For real?"

"It was terrible," said Caitlin.

Sam shifted uncomfortably on the couch. He suddenly felt even more out of place than before but couldn't pinpoint why. It wasn't like *he'd* been a county leader who decided the Black kids couldn't go to school with the white kids, but sitting in the Thomases' living room, he suddenly felt guilty by association. It was like they'd all waded into the deep end of a pool.

This wasn't just some history lesson for Jason and his mom. Just like Mrs. Baines back at the Moton Museum, Mrs. Thomas's mother had been one of the students who had protested. They had shut her out of school just because her skin was a different color. For the Thomases, it was more than it just not being fair—it was personal. Sam may not have fully realized the significance of what they'd been searching for.

"I just had a thought." Mrs. Thomas held an index finger in the air. "I've been meaning to bring the kids out to Momma's grave for a while. But you know how it is, things keep coming up, and suddenly we haven't been for years. But this picture is speaking to me."

"What's it saying?" asked Derek.

Mrs. Thomas chuckled. "That maybe now is the perfect time. She's resting out near where you three live, actually."

"She's buried at Hollywood Cemetery?" asked Derek. "We've been there a lot."

She shook her head. "There aren't many people of color buried at Hollywood. She's over at Evergreen Cemetery in the East End. My father's family was from Richmond, and she's laid next to him."

"Have I ever been?" asked Jason.

"Not since you were Angie's age. The place is overgrown and hasn't been kept up properly. It hurts to see Black folks' final resting places in such disrepair. I couldn't bring myself to go." She looked up. "But maybe now's the time. Would you like to see Granny and Grandpa Cartwright's grave?"

Jason hesitated, but then nodded. "Sure, I guess."

Sam shifted forward to the edge of the couch. It seemed like they'd done everything they'd come for. Talking about going to see their grandma's grave seemed like more of a private family matter. "We should probably be going."

"You know," Mrs. Thomas said, smiling. "You three might find it interesting to come along. I mean, with your research project and all. Evergreen's quite the historic place in its own right. Some very important Richmond leaders are buried there, even though it hasn't received its fair share of loving."

Caitlin's eyes lit up. "That would be so interesting. I've never been there."

Mrs. Thomas seemed to notice Sam's discomfort. "Only if you'd like to, of course."

He realized she was looking at him and knew he should say something. "I don't know. That sounds kind of personal. We wouldn't want to impose."

"She asked us, Sam," said Derek.

Mrs. Thomas smiled. "That's what life is, honey. Personal. And I wouldn't mind at all. Sometimes I think if we all made a little more effort to understand each other personally, this world might not be in the mess that it's in. We might be a little more loving to each other, don't you think?"

Sam nodded. If she really wanted them to go, it would be interesting to see another historic cemetery. "Thanks, if you're sure."

Caitlin glanced at her phone and made a face. "Oh, I didn't see these texts. My dad wants to know where we are. I think he's been waiting for us over at the university." She looked at Sam and Derek. "We need to go."

"No worries." Mrs. Thomas picked up the photo from the table. "May I keep this?"

"Yes, definitely," Caitlin replied. "We have copies, and I think it deserves to be here with you." On the way out of the room, Caitlin pointed at the frames on the wall. "I love your paintings. Jason said you're an artist?"

Mrs. Thomas nodded. "Thank you. I'm trying to be. It's mostly a hobby, but I've had a few small showings over at Longwood and other places in town."

"My dad is a photographer. That's how he got connected with the *Freedom Now* project in the first place."

"I'd love to meet your folks. Maybe they can come along next weekend." Mrs. Thomas reached into a basket next to the front door and pulled out a pale green business card. "Here's my email address and phone number if it works out that you can come along with us to the cemetery. I think we could plan on next weekend."

"Sounds great," said Derek. "Thanks again."

"Bye," said Sam as they walked out onto the porch.

"It's been so nice meeting you," said Mrs. Thomas. "Thank you for the photo."

"You too," said Caitlin.

Mrs. Thomas nudged Jason. "See ya," he added.

As they walked off the porch, little Angie's voice sounded behind them. "How come they're using bikes, not cars, Mommy? That's *weird*."

Caitlin started laughing as she turned to the boys. "We did it! We found Miriam Cartwright! I can't wait to tell Natalie."

"We didn't really *find* her," said Derek. He lowered his voice to a whisper. "I mean, she isn't *alive*."

"But we connected her story." Caitlin pulled her bike

upright. "And look what's already happened. Mrs. Thomas is going to visit Miriam's grave and share some of that history with her kids. It's perfect."

"You really want to go with them next weekend?" asked Sam, strapping on his bike helmet. "It still feels like intruding."

"What's it take to get you comfortable, Sam?" said Derek. "A formal written invitation?"

Sam frowned. "No, it's just that—"

The screen door banged as Jason jumped off the porch and ran over to them. "Hey, thanks for keeping quiet about the river. Mom would flip if she knew I was down there hangin' with DeShawn, even though he's my cousin. She thinks it's a bad crowd and I promised my dad I wouldn't. It was stupid anyhow; I really should have been practicing ball if I want to make the team."

"Your secret's safe with us," said Derek.

"Do you get to talk with your dad much, with him being so far away?" asked Sam.

"Sure," Jason answered, staring up the street. "He emails and stuff. We try to do a video call at least once a week when he's at the base. But it's kinda stressful."

"Will he be home soon?" asked Caitlin.

"We're hoping by Christmas, but you never know." Jason stuck his thumbs in his shorts pockets and looked back at them. "So, are you gonna come to that cemetery?"

"We'll have to ask our parents," said Caitlin. "But it sounds interesting."

"Sam needs a written invitation," mocked Derek.

Jason looked confused. "Huh?"

"Is it okay with you?" asked Sam.

"Sure, why not? I guess I've been there, but I don't really remember."

Caitlin's phone buzzed and she typed a quick reply. "That's my dad again. We really need to go."

"Hopefully we'll see you next week," said Derek.

Jason waved. "Later."

They turned and started riding away until Jason shouted again. "Hey, Sam! Hold up!"

Sam stopped pedaling and saw Jason holding something in his hand.

"I nearly forgot. Thought you might want these."

Sam's jaw dropped. "My glasses! Where did you find them?"

"After you left, I nearly stepped on them in a clump of mud next to the water. They just missed landing on a rock. I picked them up and rinsed them off, but I never expected to be giving them back to you."

Sam inspected them in the sunlight. "They don't seem broken."

"That's amazing," said Caitlin, looking over his shoulder.

Jason nodded. "Yeah, the mud must have broken the fall."

Sam slipped them on and quickly noticed the difference in the distance detail. As much as he'd rather not have to wear them, they really seemed to help. "Wow, thanks. I really appreciate it."

"I guess it's good that we ran into you after all," said Derek.

"Twice," said Jason, laughing.

Sam grinned. "Yeah, I guess so."

CHAPTER TWELVE

T he truck's tires splashed through the puddles that lingered in potholes on the pavement as they turned onto a thickly wooded road off the highway. They passed a sign that read "Historic Evergreen & East End Cemeteries."

"There's two cemeteries here?" asked Derek.

"Looks like it." Mr. Murphy slowly followed the curve in the road.

Sam stared out the window into the dense woods. He didn't see much evidence of a cemetery—at least not the kind he'd been to before, like Hollywood or St. John's Church.

"Mrs. Thomas said it's become overgrown from years of neglect, remember?" said Caitlin.

That had been an understatement based on Sam's view out the window. Tall grass grew up along the roadside in front of a thick, wild-looking forest. Dark green vines wound their way up the trunks of the trees like something out of a fairy tale.

As they continued down the road, he caught faint glimpses of cockeyed gray stones, twisted metal railings, and crumbling concrete steps. It was like an ancient civilization had been abandoned hundreds of years ago, and the vegetation had just taken over.

"Are you sure this is the right place?" asked Sam. "Everything looks really old."

"Maybe it is. I don't know if they still hold burial services," said Caitlin.

"They must have had them not too long ago," said Derek. "Isn't that why we came? Because Miriam Cartwright is buried here? Mrs. Thomas said that was only five years ago."

"I guess we'll find out soon," said Mr. Murphy, turning toward a few marked visitor parking spots near the end of the road. They parked next to a few other vehicles on a circular driveway that looped an open field. Scattered grave markers stuck out here and there like dull-colored Easter eggs hidden in the tall grass.

"There's Jason," said Derek, pointing to the Thomas family unloading from a car.

"Hey guys!" Caitlin waved and walked over.

Angie glanced up at them and then back at her mom before finally speaking to Caitlin. "You're here too? That's so *weird.*"

Mrs. Thomas sighed. "I told you we were meeting

the kids here, honey. We're going to talk about Granny Foster."

"Oh, yeah," Angie said. "I forgot."

Jason nodded at them. "What's up?" He seemed happier to see them today than he had the last time.

"Hey," said Sam. "This is quite a place."

"Thanks for letting us tag along," said Mr. Murphy after Caitlin had introduced him to Mrs. Thomas. "I hope it's not too much of an imposition."

"It's no bother at all. It was my idea, actually. The kids were so great to show me the picture of my momma. It was wonderful to see that image of her back then. And I believe Caitlin said you're involved with that project as well?"

Mr. Murphy nodded and explained how he'd worked with Natalie.

"Mrs. Thomas is an artist, too," said Caitlin.

"Is that right?" asked Mr. Murphy. "What mediums do you work in?"

"Oil paint, mostly. It's a passion I learned from Momma. But I'm still working on dedicating enough time to make it more than just a side hustle at the moment. It doesn't pay the bills as well as working as a clinical researcher, I'm afraid."

Mr. Murphy peered into the surrounding trees. "I could get some incredible shots out here."

"Did you bring your camera?" asked Derek.

Caitlin chuckled. "He brings his camera everywhere."

Mr. Murphy shrugged. "Occupational hazard, I suppose. Never want to be caught shorthanded."

"I always have mixed feelings about this place. My parents are both across the field there." Mrs. Thomas pointed to a cleared area at the other end of the grassy field. "But we nearly lost most of this to time. It's tragic really—all these folks of color deserve dignity even after they've gone."

Angie tugged on Mrs. Thomas's shirt impatiently. "Where's Granny Foster, Mommy? Didn't you say we were going to visit her?"

Jason shook his head. "Angie, she's not really here. She's—"

His mom quickly held up a hand and gave him a look. "Don't. I'll talk to her. Let's start walking around the loop."

As they followed the pavement around the curve of the field, Sam stared into the closest section of woods. It looked like some restoration work had already occurred there—much of the brush and vines had been cleared from along the ground. Some ivy still clung to the trees, but it was brown and dying. Concrete dividers like street curbs split the sections into squares.

"I think those must be different family plots," said Caitlin. Some had low metal railings, others had random sections of fencing that had become twisted. Still others were open with a scattered collection of stone grave markers inside their square.

"Look up there," said Derek. "It's like a jungle back

past the part they've cleared. I feel like we should dig through with a machete and forge a trail."

Sam glanced at Jason and shook his head. "That's how we usually get ourselves into messes, just like under the bridge."

"Yeah. Me too, I guess," he said quietly so his mom wouldn't hear. "I should have known better than to follow DeShawn down to the river. Four years' difference in age didn't use to matter when we were little. We hung out all the time. But things are different now. He's always with Brennan and those other guys you met. It's not usually a good scene."

"You said he's your cousin?" asked Sam.

"Yeah. But my aunt's always working, and he never really knew his dad, so DeShawn's basically been on his own since middle school. My mom tried to get him to stay with us a few years ago, but he kept sneaking out. She didn't like that, so now he pretty much hangs with his friends and gets into trouble. He got busted last year for stealing some canoes down at the river. The judge let him off with a warning but said next time he'd go to juvie, or maybe even a regular jail since he's so close to eighteen." He shook his head. "It's a mess."

"Sounds like your mom is right," said Caitlin. "You should stay away from him."

Jason bobbed his head. "It's complicated with family, you know?" As they reached the turn in the driveway loop, Mrs. Thomas stepped into the grass and stopped at two modest, gray stones.

Mr. Murphy motioned for them to stay on the pavement as Jason joined his family by the graves. "Let's give them a moment of privacy."

After a couple of minutes, Mrs. Thomas turned and waved to them. "Please, come join us."

Sam walked over and leaned forward to read the inscriptions on the stones:

Miriam Louise Cartwright Foster. April 17, 1947 - November 3, 2015. The stone next to hers read: *Carl Lawrence Foster. September 30, 1939 - January 5, 1996.* Sam realized that Miriam was a lot younger than her husband, and also that he'd died over twenty years ago.

"It's been nearly five years since I've last seen them," said Mrs. Thomas. "I was barely older than Jason the first time I stood here after my father passed. It was just Momma and my two brothers after that. But you find a way to make it through, just like the three of us have." She gave Jason's hand a squeeze and glanced out into the distance. "Time hasn't been good to this place."

"It looks like they're making some restoration efforts," said Mr. Murphy. As if on cue, the sound of a chainsaw roared somewhere in the distance.

Mrs. Thomas nodded. "I think so. It's long overdue. Over twenty thousand souls rest out there in those trees."

Sam felt shivers as Mrs. Thomas said that. He didn't like to think about lost souls and ghosts looming between the trees.

"Would you like to see some of the historic graves?" asked Mrs. Thomas.

"We'd love to," said Caitlin.

"I want my juice," said Angie, running in circles around her mother's legs. "I'm thirsty."

"Angie, come on, will ya?" muttered Jason. He stepped back just as Angie unexpectedly ran behind him. Her foot caught on his leg and she tumbled onto the driveway. When she saw that her knee was scraped and red, she began crying.

Mrs. Thomas gave Jason a look.

"What? I did not do that. She tripped."

Mrs. Thomas pulled Angie into her arms and tried to console her. "I'm going to have to take her to the car to clean this. I don't think I brought any bandages."

"I have some in the truck if you'd like one," offered Mr. Murphy.

Angie nodded her head quickly. "I need a Band-Aid, Mommy."

Mrs. Thomas sighed. "Thank you. That would be helpful." She turned and pointed up the hill. "Why don't you kids head up to the historic arch and see Miss Maggie's grave. I'll meet you there once we get calmed down."

"Miss Maggie?" asked Derek.

Mrs. Thomas smiled. "You'll see."

CHAPTER THIRTEEN

A s they followed the trail to the edge of the field, Jason shook his head. "Little sisters are so annoying."

Derek reached out and pushed Sam toward the weeds at the edge of the path. "Little brothers aren't much better." Sam caught his balance and shoved Derek back harder.

Jason glanced at them with his eyebrows raised. "You're both lucky to have a brother so close to your age."

Caitlin stepped ahead of them with her hands on her hips. "I think you're all lucky. I'd love to have a brother or a sister."

"Maybe," said Jason. "I guess you just get used to whatever you have."

The trail curved toward the back of the cemetery beneath a shaded section of trees. It was better maintained than what they'd seen from the road driving in, but it was still spooky. Sam glanced back at the open field to make sure he remembered which way they'd entered. The tangled mix of branches, leaves, and ivy created odd shadows and patches of light. They approached several larger graves, one prominently marked with a large stone cross. "Walker" was carved into the concrete step along the ground that divided the plot section.

Sam stared down at a square grave marker a few feet from the cross. "Maggie L. Walker. 1867-1934. At Rest." He looked up at Caitlin. "Maggie Walker? Like the school?" He knew there was a high school in Richmond by that name, but like a lot of the schools in the area, he didn't really know where the name had come from.

"Come to see Miss Maggie's grave?" a voice called out from the shadows. For an instant, Sam thought it had come from the gravestone. He stepped back with a start and saw a Black couple sitting quietly on a stone bench. One of the grave markers had been blocking them from view when they'd walked up.

"Oh, I'm sorry, we didn't mean to disturb you," said Caitlin.

The woman leaned forward and gently rose from the bench. "You're not disturbing anyone, dear. My husband here was about to doze off anyhow." She nodded at the man still seated on the bench. "That's Marvin. I'm Lucille Gibson."

Mr. Gibson rose and walked up beside his wife. "I

wasn't sleeping, Lucille, I was prayin'. The Lord knows the difference, and I'd think after forty years, you would too."

"His diabetes medication makes him tired sometimes," she whispered to them. "And he gets a little short after he's been napping."

"I may have diabetes, but there's nothin' wrong with my ears, Lucille." Mr. Gibson frowned at his wife but then gave the kids all a wide smile.

"Do *you* know who Maggie Walker was?" asked Derek.

"I think she fought for women's rights," said Caitlin, "didn't she?"

Mrs. Gibson nodded. "Oh yes. Miss Maggie was special. A pioneer, really. I suppose she's most famous for being the first Black woman to start a bank, but she did so much for Black folks here in Richmond, particularly for women." She gave Caitlin a wink. "She focused on setting folks up to succeed in life. Remember, women's suffrage didn't happen until 1920 with the Nineteenth Amendment."

"What were they suffering from?"

"Not suffering, Derek," said Caitlin quietly. "Suffrage. It's the right to vote."

Derek frowned. "Why don't they just call it that?"

"Miss Maggie was an entrepreneur—she also started a newspaper and a department store where Black folks were welcome to shop and actually try clothes on, unlike in the white stores. But she's by no means the only prominent figure resting here." Mrs. Gibson pointed across the path. "Over there is another civil rights leader, John Mitchell, Jr., editor of the powerful newspaper, *The Richmond Planet*. Dr. Sarah Garland Boyd Jones, who was one of the first Black women doctors, and the educator Dr. Andrew Bowler are here, and thousands more that we might not know about. All of whom left legacies in their own right."

"There's so much history," said Caitlin.

"Be nice if they took care of it," said Jason, starting around. "Makes me kinda mad."

"I agree, young man," said Mr. Gibson. "Black folks couldn't be buried in the white cemeteries like Hollywood or Oakwood, so they opened Evergreen in 1891. Some souls buried here were from the first generation to be born free of slavery, but they still had a long fight ahead of them."

Mrs. Gibson stared out at the graves. "When I was a girl, our family used to come here for picnics on Sundays after church. It'd be an opportunity to gather with family and friends, but we also helped to maintain the graves and keep them respectable. That practice faded over the years, and as you can see, things have really fallen apart."

"Why wouldn't the city keep it maintained?" asked Caitlin.

Mr. Gibson grunted. "Why do you think? These are mostly Black folks buried out here. Back then, not so unlike today, they were often forgotten about. But folk are resilient, and things are looking up, I'm happy to say.

A nonprofit purchased both these cemeteries, and they're working hard to bring them back. Raising millions to make it happen, actually."

"It's a blessing to see hundreds of folk volunteering to work to clear things out," said Mrs. Gibson. "Folks of all colors and ways of life, mind you. It's important for this place to regain some dignity. Make it somewhere families can come back and remember, to discover their past and honor their loved ones."

"That's so great," said Caitlin.

Sam eyed the thick vines hanging from the trees in the distance and grimaced. "There's a lot of work to do."

Mr. Gibson nodded, but then looked him straight in the eye. "There's always a lot of work to do, son. We've come a long way, but we must remember to not give up the fight."

"We were visiting my granny's grave over there." Jason pointed back to the open grassy area. "She was part of the protests for civil rights when her school was closed."

Mrs. Gibson's face brightened. "That's wonderful to hear. Would you believe that Marvin was one of the first students to integrate his high school?"

"You were in Farmville?" asked Sam.

The man shook his head. "No, I attended school in New Kent, a little east of here."

"Did they close your schools down too?" asked Derek.

"No, our school was part of a lawsuit that ultimately

112

went to the Supreme Court. In response, New Kent cooked up something called Freedom of Choice, which allowed families to decide which school they'd attend. Before that, I'd gone to the Black school, and I was one of only a few students that switched."

"That must have been exciting," said Derek. "I mean, to be the first to do something new like that."

Mr. Gibson raised his eyebrows. "Exciting wouldn't be the first word I'd use to describe it. You see, none of the white students chose to change to the Black school. And I didn't want to do it either, but my father encouraged me. He was a preacher, you know, and he told me it was important for the future. He said he believed it was God's will. I knew better than to argue with my father, or the Almighty for that matter, so I went."

"He was right," said Caitlin.

Mr. Gibson nodded. "Yes, but it was hard to see that in the moment. Being at the new school was difficult. I was an excellent student, near the top of my class at my old school, but my new teacher made it clear that things were going to be different."

"What do you mean?" asked Jason.

"On one of the first days, the teacher tells me flat-out that she doesn't want me there. Said she doesn't agree with Freedom of Choice, and that no matter how hard I work, I'll never get higher than a C in her class."

"No way," said Jason.

Caitlin shook her head. "That's awful. How could she do that?"

113

Mr. Gibson shook his head slowly. "Like I said, it was difficult times. My father encouraged me every day to keep staying the course, but I didn't like it. There was a lot of discrimination. I'll be seventy next March, but I was just seventeen in 1968 when Dr. King was killed. I was at school and this white boy —someone I knew, mind you—comes up to me at the water fountain in the school hallway. He said to me, 'Hey, Marvin. We got your daddy, and you're next.'"

"Oh my gosh." Sam's eyes opened wide.

"They were hard times," said Mrs. Gibson, patting her husband's shoulder.

Mr. Gibson nodded and looked at Derek. "So, to answer your question, no, I didn't find it exciting. Most days I was scared to death. But the Lord gave me strength and we continued on."

"That's an amazing story," Mrs. Thomas said from behind them. Everyone had been so engrossed in what the couple was saying that no one had noticed her, Angie, and Mr. Murphy walk up.

"This is my mom," said Jason.

"It's good to see young people learning about our history and coming to pay respect to their people," said Mrs. Gibson. "My parents are resting here too."

Sam glanced around at the nearby graves. He figured Mrs. Gibson's parents must be one of the nearby sets of stones. "Which ones are theirs?"

Mrs. Gibson pursed her lips. "Out there, someplace."

She nodded at the trees, a hopeless expression on her face.

"You don't know where they are?" asked Jason.

"I'm afraid the land has overtaken them," explained Mr. Gibson. "Lucille and I moved to South Carolina to start a family after we were married. Lived in a little town just outside of Spartanburg for many years. We moved back to Richmond three years ago when I retired and the kids had all moved away."

Mrs. Gibson nodded. "It just felt right to come back to our roots, where our families were from. But all those years away meant nobody came around here to maintain the graves. Lord knows the state or the city wasn't gonna do it, and this place has no perpetual care built in to the plot fees. Best I can recall, their plot was down the slope there a ways, but it's too hilly and overrun now for us to climb around and look."

"We don't get around too well now on account of my diabetes," added Mr. Gibson. "Besides, it's all just a tangle of ivy, vines, and trees."

"So why are you here?" asked Derek.

"We come mostly to remember," said Mrs. Gibson. "We may not be sitting right beside them, but we know they're somewhere close. We usually sit a spell here at Miss Maggie's grave. It's as good a place as any, and it does the soul good to remember all she did. It also reminds me of coming here as a little girl."

Sam couldn't tell if that was a sweet story, or the saddest thing he'd ever heard. He gazed out into the thick trees, realizing how tragic it was that things had become so overgrown and lost at the cemetery.

"What were their names?" asked Derek. "Maybe we can find their graves."

"Well, I don't know…" Mrs. Gibson stared out through the trees. "My father was Harold May, and Momma's name was Camille. But we were just reminiscing. I don't expect you to go find anything out there. It's too far gone, I'm afraid."

Derek nudged Jason and grinned. "What do you think?"

"Um, I guess we could look around."

Sam looked at Caitlin and sighed. He'd known it would only be a matter of time until they ended up on another wild goose chase thanks to one of his brother's hair-brained ideas.

"Just stay close," said Mr. Murphy. "I'll be right over here taking some pictures."

Mrs. Thomas glanced back at the field. "I think I'll walk with Angie back along the loop."

"Just please be careful, kids," said Mrs. Gibson.

CHAPTER FOURTEEN

A s they stepped off the gravel path behind Maggie Walker's grave, it felt like the forest had swallowed them. A few trees and branches had been cut down across the first few yards into the woods, but after that, it seemed like no one had touched the place for decades. He had that sense again, like he'd had when they drove in, that they'd entered the land that time forgot.

They walked along not so much of a path, but a trail that might have been little more than what animals used to get through the woods. The ground sloped down gently, and everything around them was green. Lush ivy spread across the ground like a blanket, but it also clung to the tree trunks and branches like it was determined to take over, choking anything in its path. It didn't take much imagination to think the entire landscape was alive and moving. Seemingly random headstones and hints of graves jutted from the ground. It was eerily quiet and still.

Sam thought about what Mr. Gibson had said, that some people buried back here were from the first generation free from slavery. Some might even have been born enslaved. Although the more they learned about Jim Crow, the more Sam realized living in those times was hardly like being completely free.

"Oh, no. Is that what I think it is?" Caitlin pointed to a single stone cross on a square marble block halfway down the slope. Three fallen headstones were laying at odd angles around it, half-buried in the ivy. Someone had sprayed red paint along the side of two of the stones.

"Looks like graffiti," said Derek.

"That's even worse than what was done to the bridge." Caitlin folded her arms angrily, but then glanced over at Jason. "Sorry, I didn't mean it like that."

Jason shrugged. "I know. I don't like it when they do that either. But there's no reasoning with DeShawn or his friends sometimes."

Sam leaned down and tried to read the inscription on the stones. "'*Stella Elizabeth Wells. March 2, 1863 - October 20, 1929. Loving Wife and Mother.*' That's nearly a hundred years ago."

"She was born right in the middle of the Civil War." Caitlin pointed to the bottom part of the stone. "'Whatsoever her hand found to do, she did it with all her might.' That's so beautiful, but also so tragic that it's lost out here in the woods like this."

A loud motor rang out through the trees. Sam couldn't tell if it was a dirt bike racing through the woods or some kind of worker's equipment. "Where's that coming from?"

"I think it's over here," said Derek. "Let's check it out."

"But what about Mr. Gibson's parents?" asked Caitlin.

Jason peered all around them and shook his head. "I think he was right. This might be a hopeless cause. We'd need a map or something."

"Or a GPS," said Derek as he jogged off to the right and toward the noise.

A flash of movement caught Sam's eye in the other direction, and he heard a rustling sound. He stepped forward cautiously and saw something moving between the trees. For an instant, he froze, remembering what Mrs. Thomas had said about lost souls, but then he spotted the tan fur of a deer inching out from behind a tree. It was just a fawn and still had its spots. It walked on thin, wobbly legs and didn't seem to notice that he was watching.

"Sam, are you coming?" Caitlin called from further up the hill. He waved his hand without taking his eyes off the fawn. There was something magical about standing that close to the baby deer, barely the size of a large dog. It seemed like he could reach out and touch it or scoop it up in his arms if he wanted to.

He glanced around. Where was its mother? It seemed

odd for it to be alone in the woods. He trailed the tiny deer further into the trees, moving slowly so as not to frighten it. When it stopped walking and turned to him, he didn't really think about the fact that he was reaching out his hand. The fawn seemed to think that maybe he had food, because it stretched its neck toward Sam's hand for a nibble.

The moment the fawn's wet black nose touched his finger, a motor screamed out through the trees behind them. The deer sprang into the air, nearly landing in Sam's arms. Then it darted down the slope toward a ravine like it had springs in its legs, dodging trees like a slalom skier.

It all happened in a flash, but Sam turned toward the noise and realized it wasn't a dirt bike motor that they'd heard, but a chainsaw. At the same time, a harsh crack followed the engine's roar as a wide tree limb crashed toward the ground twenty feet up the slope. Sam stepped back, but his leg caught on one of the iron bars that marked some of the grave plots that had been hidden deep beneath the ivy. He stumbled, landing hard at the start of the slope to the ravine. He glanced back to see a tall man walking toward him from the base of the tree. A mask covered his face and he held a chainsaw in the air, like a slasher film come to life.

The soft ground at the edge of the slope gave way under Sam's feet as he moved to stand. One moment he was on the edge of the slope, the next the dirt was gone, and he was tumbling forward into the ravine. Sam slid down, landing hard in a mix of dirt and ivy. A gnarly collection of tangled tree roots stuck out above his head, recently revealed by the landslide of earth. Just below his feet he saw a thin stream that wound along the center of the ravine.

Sam lay there for a minute, shocked at what had happened. The fawn was gone. He bent his arms and legs —nothing seemed broken. Had he imagined the figure walking toward him in the woods with the chainsaw? He pushed himself up to see around the cluster of roots, his face inches away from a rounded stone, pale and gray. He reached up to grab hold of a root to pull himself out, but more of the dirt came loose and the stone rolled on top of him. Except it wasn't a stone. Sunken holes stared back at him from a human skull.

Sam screamed and tried to scramble away. It felt like the dead had come to life and were chasing after him. As he rose to his feet and stepped forward, the sound of cracking wood came from underneath him as his leg plunged downward. He looked around in horror as bones and skeletons were seemingly scattered all around him.

He wailed as he felt something reach out and grab his shoulder. This was the end, he knew it.

"Sam, it's all right! It's me!"

He looked up and saw Derek's arm reaching down to him. A tall, silver-haired man in a red work shirt stood over Derek's shoulder. Safety goggles rested on the man's forehead and a dust mask was pulled down around his neck. Sam shuddered and stood up as Derek helped him out of the hole.

"What are you doing down there, Sam?" Derek asked, as Sam brushed off the dirt and who knew what else from his clothes.

"I was following a deer," Sam stuttered, "and then the tree fell, and I tripped, and the edge of the hill collapsed. I fell down there…" He stared back down in the hole in the ground. "Are those… skeletons?"

The chainsaw man stepped closer and knelt at the edge of the depression in the ground. "Looks like you stumbled into a grave." He glanced back at Sam. "You some kind of deviant? We've had problems with those lately."

"What?" Sam had a hard time listening. His mind had nearly shut down after the man had said he'd fallen into a grave.

"We're not vandals," Derek said. "We were just looking around." He peered down at the ground. "Is that really someone's grave?"

The man seemed to believe them and nodded. "Happens from time to time. The ground back here can be unstable, especially near this ravine. Most of the graves in this area are unmarked, so you never know when one might collapse." He nodded at Sam and grunted. "First time I've seen someone fall into one like that."

Sam tried to breathe. "What do you do with them?"

"Oh, I suppose I'll let you go. You two look pretty innocent."

Sam shook his head. "No, I mean with the graves."

The man winked at them. "We have a process when human remains come undug like this. Sometimes because of erosion, or animals, or…," he searched for the right word, "folks like yourself. When that happens, they need to be respectfully re-interred. But like I said, we've had some problems with vandals, odd rituals, and thefts for years, especially over at the mausoleum, so we'll have to take care of this area quickly."

"We saw some red paint up on that cross on the hill," said Derek.

"But that wasn't us either," Sam quickly added. He didn't know why anyone would want to cause damage or mess around at a cemetery. No matter how much disrepair a cemetery might be in, it was important to respect the dead.

He shivered thinking again about where he'd fallen. Aside from being disrespectful, it was beyond creepy. He tried not to think about having that skull roll across his chest. It felt like he'd narrowly escaped being buried alive. But in trying not to think about it, it was all he could think about. He broke into a jog, eager to be out of the woods and back with their group.

"Running from something?" Jason gave Sam a funny look as he and Derek ran up to the others walking toward the cars. "You look paler than usual."

Caitlin noticed the dirt smudges on Sam's shorts. "What happened to you?"

Sam shook his head. "Don't ask."

"Sorry again that we didn't find the grave," said Jason. "You were right, it's a jungle back there."

Mr. Gibson nodded. "It was nice of you kids to try."

As they reached the cars, Jason turned to his mom. "How come Granny's all the way out here, anyway? I've seen cemeteries in Farmville. Wouldn't that have been a lot closer?"

Mrs. Thomas opened the door and Angie climbed into her car seat. "You may not know this, but my father's family came from Richmond originally. They moved out to Prince Edward County during the fifties when construction started for the new interstate highway."

Mr. Gibson's head perked up. "They lived in Jackson Ward? Lucille and I were just talking about heading over there to one of our favorite spots for lunch—a local institution called Mama J's."

Mrs. Gibson stopped and smiled. "Do ya'll like Southern soul food?"

"Um…" said Sam. "I don't know if I've ever had it."

Jason turned to his mom. "Do you make that?"

She smiled. "Sometimes. That's another thing my momma taught me."

"They've got the best catfish sandwich, add in some mashed potatoes and collard greens." Mr. Gibson licked his lips. "I can taste it now."

"Catfish?" Angie called from the open car window. "Ew!"

Mrs. Gibson laughed. "Or maybe some fried chicken with mac and cheese might be more to your liking, dear."

"Top it off with some peach cobbler for dessert," added Mr. Gibson.

Sam felt his stomach rumble at the mention of food, but didn't want to be the first to say something. Maybe soul food was a little different from the cheesesteak he'd had for lunch at the café in Farmville last week, but all the talk was making him hungry. He was ready to put his experience in the woods behind him.

Mrs. Thomas looked at Mr. Murphy and they both nodded. "Well, if you don't mind us joining you, that sounds very nice. Thank you."

"Sweet," said Sam. If there was anything that could distract him from trouble, it was a good meal.

CHAPTER FIFTEEN

S am stared up at the tall, bronze statue that stood more than twice his height.

"Maggie Lena Walker," was inscribed on the circular base. She wore a long dress, and her hand clutched a beaded necklace. He couldn't help but think from the warm smile on her face that Maggie Walker seemed like she'd have been a nice lady to know.

"It's good to see the city better representing some of the Black folk who've made such strong contributions," said Mr. Gibson, walking up with the others. "Have you seen the Arthur Ashe statue over on Monument Avenue?"

Derek shook his head. "I thought there were only Confederate monuments on that avenue."

"All but one," Mr. Gibson answered. "Arthur Ashe became one of the greatest tennis champions in the world. He was from Richmond, and appropriately, he attended Maggie Walker High School, if I recall. But right around the time of those student protests we've been talking about, he wasn't allowed to play against white players in segregated Richmond, and the city's indoor courts didn't allow Black players either."

"Even for someone as good as him?" asked Derek.

"Didn't matter," said Mr. Gibson. "So he moved away, went to St. Louis, I think. And the rest is history, as they say. I'll bet he didn't expect to be joining those Confederate generals on the avenue back when he was your age." Mr. Gibson sat on a bench and looked off into the distance. "You know, when I was a boy, the only view I had of a street like Monument Avenue was from the car. I wasn't welcome to walk down the sidewalk like I can now. The only reason to be over there was to do work, and even then, you went in through the back of the buildings. White folk caught you walking by, they'd come out and ask what you were doing there."

Mrs. Thomas walked around the plaza with Angie and read several of the curved inscriptions on the benches, each showing a point on the timeline of Maggie Walker's accomplishments. "She achieved so much. It's seeing things like this that give me a bit of hope. Sometimes things seem like they're all heading in the wrong direction." She placed her hand on the hem of the statue's long dress. "But not everything."

"The Maggie Walker House is only about three blocks from here," said Mrs. Gibson. "It's a mansion on part of what they called Quality Row, and it is now a National Park Service Historical Site."

"Is that where Miss Maggie lived?" asked Caitlin.

Mrs. Gibson nodded. "That's right. Jackson Ward was one of Richmond's most prominent African-American neighborhoods."

"They once called this area the Harlem of the South and Black Wall Street, if I remember correctly," said Mr. Murphy. "I've had several photo shoots on the blocks that remain. There's some amazing architecture. The Black History Museum on Leigh Street looks like a castle because of when it was an armory."

Mr. Gibson smiled. "Have you been to the Hippodrome Theater? It was long before my time, but my grandfather used to tell me about going to shows there in the twenties. The Deuce—that's what they called Second Street back then—was hopping with performers like Billie Holiday, Louis Armstrong, Duke Ellington, and Cab Calloway. There's a statue to Bill 'Bojangles' Robinson a few blocks from here too."

Jason turned to his mom. "Didn't you say at the cemetery that Grandpa Foster's family was from Jackson Ward?"

Mrs. Thomas nodded. "That's right. But they moved to Prince Edward County during the fifties when construction started for the new interstate highway."

"The Richmond-Petersburg Highway," said Mr. Gibson. He leaned out toward them. "Better known today as I-95."

"Why did they have to move because of the highway?" asked Sam. "Was it too noisy?"

"They should have built some of those big, concrete sound barriers," said Derek.

Mr. Gibson chuckled. "That might have worked if there were any homes left to keep the sound out from."

Jason raised his eyebrows. "What do you mean?"

"Well," said Mrs. Thomas. "My father's home was bulldozed, just like hundreds of others."

"They can just do that?" asked Caitlin.

Mr. Gibson nodded. "Highways have got to go somewhere, sure, but it was easy pickings to select the thriving Black neighborhood for the location, and eminent domain rarely gave fair market value. That highway cut a path straight through the neighborhood, a block wide, as if a twister had set down in the middle of town and wiped everything away. And don't get me started about the convention center and that butt-ugly coliseum that tries to act like a sports arena."

"Marvin, your language," scolded Mrs. Gibson.

The man frowned and looked back at them. "I apologize, but it's true."

Sam tried to imagine what having a neighborhood cut in half by an interstate highway would do to the feel of the streets and the people that lived there. It did sound kind of like ripping the heart out of a community. He noticed a woman moving along the sidewalk, handing out bright yellow flyers to all the passersby. She walked closer and handed a paper to Jason. Before he could read it, Angie snatched it from him and held it out proudly for everyone to see. "Look what that lady gave me, Mommy!"

Mrs. Thomas opened it up and read. "Families for social justice rally."

"I read about that in the newspaper," said Mr. Murphy. "It's at the capitol, right?"

"It's just like Barbara Johns," said Caitlin.

"And Granny Foster," Jason added. "We should go see it. You know, be a part of something like that and not just learn about it."

"It's an interesting thought," said Mrs. Thomas, reading the fine print on the flyer. "It's next Saturday on the capitol steps."

"We could come too," exclaimed Derek. "I mean, if that would be okay with everybody."

Mr. Murphy nodded. "It's okay with me, but you boys will need to ask your parents. Actually, I'm traveling out of town for a photo shoot in Norfolk next weekend, so they might need to drive all three of you."

"I don't mean to be rude, but I think we said something about going to lunch, didn't we?" said Derek.

Mrs. Gibson laughed. "You're right, young man. Good eats are just around the corner."

"Did I mention the cornbread?" Mr. Gibson shook his head. "Mama J's has the best cornbread."

"Well, what are we waiting for?" asked Mrs. Thomas. "Lead the way!"

CHAPTER SIXTEEN

Crowds were already gathered in the blocks surrounding the Virginia State Capitol when Sam, Derek, and Caitlin arrived with the boys' parents. They'd parked several blocks away and walked up Ninth Street toward the capitol square in downtown Richmond.

"Looks like we're at the right place," said Derek, waiting at the intersection for the light to turn. "Seems like half the state is here today."

"I expect there may be several different rallies happening today," said Mom.

"The General Assembly is holding a special session this week, and it's brought people out of the woodwork to support various causes," explained Dad.

"Like civil rights?" asked Sam.

"Like all kinds of things," said Caitlin. "My parents were telling me there's legislation up for discussion about everything from guns to solar energy, prison reform, and even more."

"Just remember what we talked about in the car," said Dad.

"That exercising our right to free speech is one of the most important things we can do?" asked Sam.

"I thought voting was the most important?" added Derek.

"Both of those things are true," said Dad. "But just watch yourselves. Rallies like this can draw all kinds of people. Everyone's not always rallying for the same side of the cause as you are."

Derek put his hands on his hips. "You guys always say we should stand up for the truth. Some things are worth fighting for, right?"

Dad nodded. "Of course, but God put a brain in that head that's sitting on your shoulders too, don't forget. There's nothing wrong with being smart *and* standing up for what's right. I'm sure most folks are here because they truly believe in a cause and want their voices heard, but others sometimes just like to have their voices heard, if you know what I mean."

Sam looked across the sidewalk at his brother and nodded. "Yeah, I know someone like that."

Derek made a face like he was insulted.

"So what your father is saying is that you need to stay together," added Mom. "And be mindful of who you're with."

"You don't think things will be violent, do you?" asked Caitlin.

"Not likely," said their dad. "But it never hurts to stay alert." He stopped walking at the corner of the capitol square and looked them each in the eye. "Understood?"

"Yes, sir," answered Caitlin.

He raised his eyebrows. "Boys?"

"Yes, Dad," they both replied.

Derek peered up ahead. "Now, where should we go first?"

"Aren't we supposed to meet up with Jason and his family?" Sam looked around for any signs about the social justice rally. There were so many people coming and going, it was hard to tell what was what.

Caitlin checked her phone. "I think we're a few minutes earlier than we said we'd meet. Let's walk around the capitol grounds in the meantime." She glanced at Sam's parents. "Is that okay?"

Their dad nodded. "Just stay in the capitol square. I don't want you wandering off around the city. I think the rally will be up on the capitol steps at 10:30. We'll look for you there."

"Got it, Dad," said Derek. He waved them up the hill. "Come on."

Caitlin gazed around the square with excitement and pointed up at the stately capitol building at the top of the hill. Its tall columns were so white they almost sparkled in the sunlight. "You know that Thomas Jefferson designed the capitol, right? He modeled it after a Roman temple."

Sam remembered from their tour of Monticello and Poplar Forest how much Jefferson had loved designing buildings. "And he was the governor, too, wasn't he?"

Caitlin grinned. "Good memory."

"So he lived right there?" asked Derek.

She shook her head. "When he started as governor, the capital was still in Williamsburg, but I think it moved to Richmond in his second term. Have you seen the governor's mansion? It's right up there." She pointed up the hill at a building flanked by tall, leafy trees.

"He got a mansion?" exclaimed Derek. "Maybe I should be governor."

"They might let you paint the deck," muttered Sam, marveling at his brother's lofty opinion of himself.

Sam saw a towering statue on horseback up ahead. "Is that George Washington?"

"He wasn't governor too, was he?" asked Derek.

Caitlin chuckled. "No, but he was from Virginia. Remember going to Mount Vernon?"

"Oh, right." Derek grinned. "I knew that."

Caitlin stopped in her tracks as they walked past the Washington statue. She stared to their left with her mouth open. "Oh my gosh!"

"What's wrong?" asked Sam.

"Look!" She pointed and ran across the grass.

"Another statue," moaned Derek. "Awesome. Didn't you say something about a mansion?"

Sam didn't know what had her so excited, but when he saw what she was staring at, it all made sense.

"It's Barbara Johns!" Caitlin exclaimed. In front of them stood a life-sized statue of a young Barbara Johns leading a group of students. The granite wall behind them was inscribed, "It seemed like reaching for the moon."

"It's in memory of the student strike in Farmville," said Caitlin. "I saw those words at the Moton Museum. Barbara said their goals seemed so far away, it was like trying to touch the moon."

Derek walked around the side of the wall. "Hey, look, there's more!"

The piece turned out to be a four-sided monument dedicated to civil rights. Barbara and the students from Moton High were on one side, another had Oliver Hill and Spottswood Robinson, the two lawyers from the NAACP who had helped fight for the *Brown* case, and yet another had L. Francis Griffin, the reverend at Farmville's First Baptist Church.

Derek stopped at the last panel, a group of six people of varying ages. "These just look like ordinary people."

Caitlin looked up at words inscribed above the statues. "It makes more sense when you read the quote. Thurgood Marshall was the first Black Supreme Court justice. Listen: 'The legal system can force open doors and sometimes even knock down walls. But it cannot build bridges. That job belongs to you and me.'"

"A job for me? That's *weird*," a small voice called out.

They turned around and saw Mrs. Thomas, Jason, and Angie smiling behind them. "Hey," said Sam. "You made it."

"We sure did," said Mrs. Thomas. "And what an appropriate place to meet up. I wanted to show the kids this monument too before we headed to the rally."

Jason said hi and walked up next to them by the statue. "That's really cool."

"Strong words, don't you think?" asked Mrs. Thomas.

"It's kind of why we're here today, right?" asked Caitlin. "Trying to work together and build bridges."

"I like to build bridges with my blocks," said Angie.

"Not that kinda bridge, Angie," muttered Jason. He shot Sam a knowing look. "She never knows how to be quiet."

Caitlin bent down. "I'll bet you do, Angie. It's good to see you again." Angie reached out and gave Caitlin a big hug. "Oh, thank you, friend!" said Caitlin.

"I like that this is here," said Jason, circling the monument. "It's better than some of the other ones." He pointed down the grass to the statue of a lone man dressed in a suit and carrying a book.

"Harry Flood Byrd," Sam read.

"Remember, Massive Resistance?" asked Caitlin.

"Oh, right," said Sam. "That's kind of ironic that they're so close to each other."

Mrs. Thomas shrugged. "You might say that. Just another reminder that history is a mixed bag. Some people bring us forward, others pull us back." She glanced at her watch. "But we'd better head around to the steps. I think the rally is going to start soon."

CHAPTER SEVENTEEN

The capitol steps were packed. Sam noticed a couple of smaller groups to the side with signs and banners of their own, but the rally for social justice was by far the largest in the capitol square. There had to be several thousand people lined up on all sides of the capitol steps, on the lawn, and even spilling down into the street.

Mrs. Thomas directed them into a spot on the grass halfway up the hill. The sun was out, but it didn't feel oppressively hot because of the gentle breeze blowing through the square.

"This is crazy!" shouted Derek. "Look at this crowd."

The police seemed to have closed off most of the road with metal barriers, leaving only the center for people to walk through. A much smaller contingent of protesters was gathered on the fringes of the main crowd and along the sidewalk across the street. They seemed to be supporting another side of the issue. Two Confederate flags had been draped over the metal barrier, and people held signs, but they were too far away for Sam to read, even with his glasses.

Sam looked back up the capitol steps and was encouraged to see that there was a healthy mix of people of all different skin colors, genders and age groups in the crowd. He noticed several groups of families with kids his age and even some younger kids like Angie. Many wore buttons or held up signs with slogans like "Justice Now," "Let your voices be heard," and "Anti-Racism." Some held up pictures of faces or names. Sam assumed they must be people who'd been mistreated or even killed because of their skin color. Most people were smiling and seemed happy to be there with so many others supporting the cause.

"You know this reminds me of another famous rally for justice," said Mrs. Thomas.

"Was it here in Richmond?" asked Caitlin.

"No, it was the March on Washington back in 1963. It's where Dr. King gave his famous 'I Have a Dream' speech at the Lincoln Memorial. I may not have been around to see it, but I still get tears in my eyes every time I hear that," said Mrs. Thomas.

"That's the same year as our picture," said Caitlin.

Mrs. Thomas nodded. "A lot was happening at that time. President Kennedy was killed just a few weeks after the march."

Sam tried to remember what he knew about that

famous speech. He'd heard clips of it in school or on TV commercials, but he mostly just remembered the phrase "I have a dream." He supposed he could use a refresher.

"Keep your ears open," Mrs. Thomas said. "They just might quote some of it here today at the rally. It's very moving."

"There's Mom and Dad." Derek waved his arms toward the edge of the crowd where he had spotted his parents. "Over here!"

They noticed Derek's waving and waded through the scores of people until they stood next to the group. "What a turnout!" exclaimed Dad.

Sam introduced everyone and they all said hello. His mom gazed out into the crowd. "We didn't know if we'd be able to find you all."

Angie tugged on Sam's mom's shirt. "You're his mom?"

Sam's mom looked down and smiled. "That's right, honey."

Angie glanced back at Sam and made a face. "That's *weird*."

Sam's parents laughed, but Mrs. Thomas put her hand over her eyes. "Angie, be nice." She looked back up at Sam's mom. "I'm so sorry, she seems to say that about everything these days."

Sam's mom laughed. "It's no problem. I'm used to never knowing what will come out of these two's mouths." She tussled Derek's hair. "Especially this one."

Derek was about to object, but a loud cheer erupted

from the crowd. A man and a woman had appeared behind a podium at the top of the steps.

"It's wonderful to see all of you here today," the woman said into a microphone. "I'll take this beautiful, clear morning as a sign of the bright future for *every* Virginian in this commonwealth."

The crowd cheered and several waved their home-made signs back and forth, reminding Sam of the signs from the Farmville protests. It was like the frozen gray photographs had come to life in living color.

A moment of silence recognized those who had lost their lives or suffered under the weight of discrimination and hatred. Then the woman, who was a state senator, introduced a minister from a local Black church in Richmond. He stepped up to the podium and called out to the crowd in a deep, captivating voice.

"These steps where we stand today have a long and checkered history. They have established liberty and freedom, and yet in the same breath fought for slavery and discrimination. For decades, brave voices of freedom shouted for a change that was far too slow to come. They are still shouting, my friends, and change is still far, far too slow in coming."

He paused as the crowd cheered in agreement. Some people even called out, "Amen."

"Today we continue the fight, the struggle, for equality and opportunity that began so long ago. We honor names like King, Hill, Johns, Morgan, Marshall, Green, Walker, Robinson, Griffin, and countless others whose struggles were in the shadows and away from the spotlight. And yet today we still fight, we still work together, people from all communities, all colors and walks of life, working together for a common cause—to end the pernicious scourge of racism and discrimination that still haunts our city, our country, and our world.

"And yet, as I gaze out across these steps, I see the thousands of you gathered here today—young and old, Black and white, men and women, all God's children, standing tall for a mighty cause that is bigger than any one of us. It fills my soul with hope, not unlike the dream envisioned by Dr. King nearly sixty years ago, that we *will* come together, that we *will* lift each other up, that we *will* show love and mercy to our fellow human beings, just as our good Lord has called us to do."

Sam was drawn in by the preacher's powerful words at the microphone. It felt like the man was speaking right to him, but also to the entire crowd. He glanced at Jason and Caitlin next to him and saw they were also in rapt attention. Even Derek seemed to be listening for a change. Sam turned to his parents behind him and smiled. It was a good thing they had come.

Half a dozen other speakers came up to the podium during the rally. Some told stories about their family members who had suffered injustices, some spoke of a loved one who had been killed. Some speakers yelled out in anger, others shed tears, and many did both. Many spoke about their African-American husbands, sons, and fathers in prison, and about how many judicial sentences seemed to discriminately impact people of color.

As things drew to a close, Sam thought the noise from the counter-protesters down on the street was louder than it had been when the rally began. Maybe it was just because there was a lull between speakers up at the podium, or maybe they chose that moment specifically to make themselves heard. Sam stood on his tiptoes and peered through the throngs of people behind them. Some of the people across the street were waving their Confederate flags and shouting. Some were arguing with people from the social justice rally.

"That doesn't sound good," said Caitlin.

Sam glanced at his dad, who raised his eyebrows and nodded.

"A consequence of free speech," said Mrs. Thomas, leaning down. "I'm afraid they have just as much right to voice their opinions as we do ours." She winked at them. "But it's good to see our numbers are larger!"

"I don't see why being racist should be legal," said Jason.

"We can't, and probably don't want to have the government policing people's thoughts and attitudes," Mrs. Thomas replied. "But there's a line to be drawn between thinking or speaking your mind and infringing on other people's rights."

A loud rumble sounded from down the block and seemed to grow in intensity. Someone waved a huge banner that read *Preserve Our Southern Heritage* and dozens of horns began honking.

Then a sinking feeling hit Sam's stomach. He had heard that noise before. A narrow line of motorcycles appeared down the middle of the road. The police were waving them along to the next block.

"Is that who I think it is?" whispered Derek, leaning over.

Sam nodded his head. He couldn't tell for sure, but he'd bet money that some, or maybe all of the guys down there on the motorcycles were from the Confederate Ghosts, the biker gang they'd run into several times on past adventures.

They'd become kind of friends with their leader, Mad Dog DeWitt, who acted more like a grandpa than a notorious biker. They'd seen the bikers rally around Confederate statues before over on Monument Avenue and at Jefferson Davis's grave in Hollywood Cemetery, but they'd usually interacted because of some kind of mystery they were solving. While he'd known some of their leather jackets and bike helmets had Confederate flags on them, Sam had never paid much attention to the group's politics.

But now, as he stared down the street at the bikes rolling past waving Confederate flags, he suddenly felt queasy.

"Can you believe that?" grumbled Jason.

The counter-protesters continued to get more vocal as the bikes progressed along the street. Mrs. Thomas picked Angie up and held her closer. "I think we're going to need to get to the car. She's already late for her nap, and I don't want her to get scared if things escalate down there."

"Mom, it's not over," argued Jason.

Mrs. Thomas nodded. "But it will be soon, and I've just stated my reasons." She smiled at Sam's parents and tugged at Jason's shirt. "So glad you all could come."

Dad looked out over the restless crowd. "Maybe we'll join you." He glanced at Caitlin and the boys. "Okay?"

"Yeah," Sam answered quickly, straining to see where the bikers were turning onto the next street. He was glad they had joined the Thomases at the rally, but this was all getting to be too much.

They followed Mrs. Thomas through breaks in the crowd until they reached the sidewalk at the bottom of the hill. Lots of people were filtering out in that same direction, and the sidewalks were full.

Sam caught sight of a long line of motorcycles parked at the curb on the next corner. He tried to blend into the crowd, but stepped a little too close to Derek, catching the back of his shoe.

"Sam, watch where you're going, will you?" Derek barked as he nearly tripped.

Derek's voice carried as always, and out of the corner of his eye, Sam saw a group of leather-clad bikers a couple yards away on the street corner. He didn't want to look up, but he couldn't help scanning their faces to see if they'd met before.

His eyes locked on a familiar face before he quickly looked back down at the sidewalk.

"Hey, look who it is!" the man shouted over the crowd. It was too late to pretend he hadn't seen him; the man was just on the other side of the curb.

Derek put his hand on Sam's shoulder. "I think he's talking to us."

The biker—Chris, Sam remembered, nudged the man in a leather jacket beside him. The tall man's back had been facing the sidewalk, but Sam knew who it was before he even turned.

It was Mad Dog.

CHAPTER EIGHTEEN

"**W**ell, I'll be darned. What's cookin', boys?" Mad Dog waved and walked closer. His voice sounded like it always did—as if he'd just swallowed a fistful of gravel.

Sam glanced up and saw that his parents, Caitlin, and even Mrs. Thomas with Angie and Jason had stopped just up the path to wait for him and Derek.

"Long time, no speak," called Mad Dog, with Chris at his side.

Derek stepped up first and shook hands with the men. Sam didn't know what else to do, so he tried to smile and did the same. He glanced over his shoulder and saw Jason staring at him. He felt even worse than when he'd been sitting in the Thomases living room. That had mostly just been confusing, but this time he felt that if Jason's stares could shoot lasers, they'd cut him in two.

Mad Dog slapped them both hard on the back and laughed. "Didn't know y'all would be here. Glad to see you boys standing up to preserve our Southern roots, although if I recall, you two are actually Yankees." He wore a sticker on his jacket with the Confederate flag and the words "Keep it Flying."

"Yeah," Sam squeaked weakly. "Something like that."

"Awesome!" Chris flashed a wide grin. "Here, have a sticker!" His arm shot out and smacked a Confederate flag sticker on Sam's chest.

Sam struggled to catch his breath, like he'd just taken a punch to the gut. "Well," he stuttered, sweat beading on his forehead. "We gotta go. See ya." He turned back to the sidewalk before either of the men could object or stick anything else on him.

"All right, take care then," Mad Dog answered, but Sam didn't turn back around. He just pulled Derek over to where everyone was waiting on the sidewalk.

"Ready to go?" Dad asked.

"Yeah." Sam discreetly reached up and tried to peel off the sticker, but it stuck to his shirt and only partially ripped off. Caitlin grimaced like she understood how he felt. The crowd was tight, and soon Sam found himself walking shoulder to shoulder with Jason. He felt his friend's eyes boring into him.

"You know those guys?" Jason asked.

"Um, kind of. It's a long story."

Caitlin came closer to help. "We met them on another adventure."

"A couple of them, actually," Derek added. "They're nice guys, believe it or not."

Jason raised his eyebrows but didn't answer. He just started walking faster and caught up with his mom and sister. By the time the group reached the next intersection and Sam's parents turned toward their car, the crowd had pulled them apart from the Thomases. Sam's parents just waved to Mrs. Thomas, and they all went on their way.

The sidewalk traffic had thinned by the time they reached the other side of the crosswalk. But Sam still felt like he was going to be sick. "I can't believe that just happened."

"I don't think it was that bad." Derek raised his hands. "A little awkward, maybe, but we do know them, Sam. Do you want to just pretend that we're not friends? You know as well as I do that Mad Dog has saved our bacon more than once. He's a good guy."

Sam shook his head. "Yeah, but they were part of the other protest. Did you see what they were doing? Waving the Confederate flag, cheering for Southern pride."

"I know what you mean." Caitlin nodded. "That was totally against what the social justice rally was about. It didn't seem right."

"Did you see how Jason was staring at me?" asked Sam. "And this stupid sticker they slapped on my shirt." He scratched at the torn edges that remained. "I couldn't get it off."

They reached the car, but when everyone was inside,

his dad didn't start the engine. He and Mom turned around in their seats. "You all okay? There was a lot going on back there."

"I assume those bikers were some of the men you've met before?" asked Mom.

"How'd you guess?" Sam muttered.

"It was Mad Dog and Chris," Caitlin explained. "We've met them a few times. Sam feels like he let the Thomases down. I think we all do."

"Is that right, Sam?" asked Dad.

Sam let out a long breath. "What's the chance that with all those thousands of people at the capitol, we had to be on the same exact sidewalk as the only Confederate biker gang that we know in the entire world?"

Derek shrugged. "Probably pretty low, although I don't know how many different Confederate biker gangs there are out there. I'll bet my phone would tell us—"

"Derek, that's enough," said Mom firmly before Sam could tell his brother what he could do with his phone.

"Fine," said Derek, "but it's not like *you* were waving the Confederate flag out there, Sam."

"It was just a misunderstanding," said Caitlin. "We all know the truth, that we were there supporting the rally for social justice. I'm sure the Thomases understood."

"I doubt it," Sam muttered. "They probably all think I'm racist, or segregationist, or whatever you'd call what the Ghosts were doing."

"Honey." Mom reached back and patted his knee. "I

think that if you're sincere about what you believe in and tell that to Jason, he'll believe you, too."

"But I will also say that actions often speak louder than words," added Dad.

"Sweetheart, I'm trying to make him feel better," said Mom.

"I know, and that was a hard lesson back there. But sometimes it's in the hardest situations that our beliefs are really put to the test."

"I hate tests," said Sam.

"Are you trying to say that Mad Dog is a bad guy and we should have been rude to him?" asked Derek. "I wasn't kidding. He really did save our butts a few times."

Dad nodded. "No doubt, seeing the situations you three have gotten yourselves into over the years. But one good, or bad, action doesn't usually tell the whole story of a person."

Caitlin nodded. "Yeah, remember Thomas Jefferson? He wrote the Declaration of Independence and yet had a relationship and kids with Sally Hemings while she was still his enslaved worker."

"So we can't celebrate anyone?" Derek moaned. "I mean, nobody's perfect."

"I don't know if it means that," answered Dad. "But I do think we should do everything we can to work for what's right. Too many people are content to fall back on keeping things how they've always been or claiming ignorance instead of doing right."

"It's each of our jobs to educate ourselves," said

Mom. "And as bad as you feel right now, today might have been a good step toward understanding someone else's perspective."

Sam gave a long sigh and looked up at his parents. "So what do I do now? I don't know if the Thomases are going to want to talk to us anymore. I feel like I betrayed them."

"Maybe give it a little time," said Mom. "But I'd suggest you reach out. If you're sincere and honest, hopefully Jason will understand."

Sam pushed his head back against the seat and closed his eyes. "I doubt it."

CHAPTER NINETEEN

The next day, Mr. Haskins put Sam to work on painting his deck. Unlike the clear weather coating that Derek had applied to their own back deck, Mr. Haskins had picked out a dark brown stain.

"It won't show the dirt as much as a natural color," their neighbor argued when Sam questioned him about it.

"What about bird poop?" Sam asked. "Wouldn't that show up even more?"

Mr. Haskins stared at him for a moment and then glanced up at the sky. "They wouldn't dare."

Luckily Mr. Haskins's deck was only about a third of the size of their deck, so Sam finished staining in only two hours. He called Mr. Haskins out to inspect as he banged the lid shut on the stain can.

The old man bobbed his head. "Not too bad, I suppose, for the first coat at least."

Sam looked up. "First coat?"

Mr. Haskins grinned. "What, you didn't think I was gonna let you off the hook that easily, did ya? We gotta give the wood time to let it seep in, get used to it a while. Come back tomorrow and it should be ready for another go. Some work takes time."

"But how many coats does it need?" Sam was almost afraid to ask.

"Oh, at least two… maybe three. Four at the most."

"Four?" griped Sam.

Mr. Haskins grinned at him. "Did I mention the lemonade?"

Sam never knew when the old man was joking or serious, but he groaned as he wrapped the brush in a plastic grocery bag and stored it under the deck with the cans. He checked his phone as he walked back down the driveway to his house. Still no response from Jason.

"All done with the deck?" Derek stopped him on the front porch.

"Maybe," Sam replied. "I might have twenty more coats to apply. Mr. Haskins is crazy."

"Still no reply from Jason?"

Sam shook his head. "I keep trying, but he won't answer or text me back."

"I have an idea."

"Your ideas are usually terrible."

Derek frowned. "Not always."

"What is it?" asked Sam, warily.

"Just watch. Give me his number."

154

"I told you, he won't answer. I've already tried. Aren't you listening?"

"Yeah, but he doesn't know my number," Derek whispered as his phone started ringing on speaker. "He might pick up."

"Hello?" a voice answered.

Derek flashed a superior look. "Jason, hey, it's Derek."

There was silence on the other line.

"We were trying to reach you, but Sam said you wouldn't answer. So I thought I'd try. How are you?"

"What do you want?" Jason replied in a monotone.

Sam leaned closer to the phone. "Hey, Jason, it's Sam. I just wanted to apologize for the other day at the rally. That didn't end well, and I wanted to explain about those bikers. I'm sure it didn't look very good."

Jason's tone changed quickly. "What do you mean? It looked fine."

Derek and Sam shot each other quick glances. "It did?"

"Sure, don't worry about it," said Jason, sarcasm now definitely showing through his voice. "You and your biker buddies just want things to stay the same. So whatever, it's cool."

"That's the problem." Sam tried to get things back on track. "We're not with them—"

"No?" Jason interrupted. "Then tell me I didn't see you palling around with a gang of Confederate sympathizers. I mean, they had flags on their jackets, man. I thought you were different, but maybe you're just part of the problem."

"What's that supposed to mean?" asked Derek.

"It's like DeShawn says—white people are all just playing on their privilege. They might talk a good game for a little while, but when things get tough, they're going to stand on the side of history. I mean, I get it. Why would you want change when you're the ones running the show?"

"That's not fair," said Derek.

"And it's not true, either," added Sam.

"I know what I saw," said Jason coldly. "Stop calling me."

The line disconnected, leaving the brothers staring at the silent phone.

"Well, that didn't go the way I thought it would," Derek muttered.

Sam felt sick. He put his hand over his face. "This is a disaster."

* * *

IT FELT like he'd been lying in the dark for hours, trying to get to sleep, but Sam glanced at his alarm clock and it was just eleven. He heard his parents walking down the hall to go to bed. One of them poked their head through his doorway.

"Goodnight," Sam whispered.

"Goodnight, son."

The door started to shut, but Sam called back out. "Dad?"

"Yeah?"

"Do you think I'm part of the problem?"

His dad came into the room and sat on the edge of the bed. "The problem?"

"That's what Jason told Derek and me on the phone. He said that we're part of the problem."

"That's a pretty rough accusation. What do you think?"

Sam shook his head. "I don't know what I could have done. I was really enjoying being at that rally, you know? I liked showing support for racial justice. But then it all got turned on its head somehow. I didn't mean to do anything racist."

His dad patted his shoulder. "I know that, Sam."

"Then what can I do? Jason hung up on me today. He said he doesn't want to talk to us anymore."

His dad was quiet for a few moments. "You know, sometimes *not* doing something can be enough to cause harm. You're right, you didn't actively do something bad or evil, but that might be the point. We all need to look for ways that we can actively help lift others up."

"What does it mean to play off our privilege?"

"Well," his dad started, "we may not always feel it, but our family has a pretty privileged history compared to some. It's easy to assume that others will be fine, that they'll figure it out, or that somehow it's their own fault they're in the spot they're in. But someone else's situation might be harder than it looks from our perspective, whether we're talking about racial justice, economic hardship, family situations, or other things."

Sam let out a long breath and tried to think it through. "But that's just it, Dad. I felt like I was noticing those kinds of things. We really are trying to help track down the people in those pictures. We didn't go to the rally to support the Confederate cause. We went with the Thomases to stand up for what was right."

"As far as I see it, that's all true," said Dad. "So, what's bothering you?"

"What's bothering me is that Jason and probably his whole family think we're actually closet racists because we're friends with Mad Dog. But I don't agree with any of that Confederate pride stuff. It just wasn't part of how we got to know the Ghosts."

"Did you tell him that?" asked Dad.

"Jason? Yes, that's what I was just explaining."

"No, I don't mean Jason."

Sam shook his head. "Dad, what are you talking about?"

"I mean, did you tell that to Mad Dog?"

"Tell him what?"

"That you were at the capitol supporting racial justice."

Now it was Sam's turn to sit quietly. "Um, no… I guess I just kind of let Mad Dog assume what he wanted to assume. And then Chris slapped that stupid sticker on my shirt."

"And why did you just let him assume?" Dad asked gently.

A light bulb finally went off in Sam's head as he saw what his dad was getting at. "Because telling him I didn't agree with him would have been awkward and hard and made me feel uncomfortable." He shifted in his bed. "Kinda like now."

Dad leaned down and squeezed him in a hug. "I think you found your answer. Sometimes doing the right thing can be uncomfortable. If it was easy, we'd likely have a lot more people doing it, and the world would be a different place." He stood up and walked toward the doorway. "It's late. Get some sleep. Things have a way of feeling better in the morning."

Sam rolled over to a cool spot on his pillow and closed his eyes. "Thanks, Dad."

CHAPTER TWENTY

The TV was on in the living room all afternoon. Which was unusual, since Jason's mom was particular about him and Angie not having too much screen time. Even more unusual was that it was turned to the news. His mom swore several times a year she wouldn't watch the news anymore because it got her too worked up. But it was on, nonetheless.

A reporter was live in downtown Richmond near a bunch of Confederate monuments. Crowds had been gathering throughout the past two days in response to violence in another city where a Black man had been killed. Now folks were standing up in cities like Richmond and all over the country to make their voices heard. They'd been marching in the streets, waving signs, and calling for justice and change. It was similar to the rally his family had attended at the capitol, but from what Jason could see on TV, these protests had a sharper edge to them. A lot of people were angry, and for good reason.

Every time his mom walked through the room, she'd pause and watch for a few minutes, mutter a few things to herself, and then walk away. He couldn't decide if she was happy or aggravated about what was happening, but it seemed like a bit of both. They'd been expecting a video call from his dad for a couple days, but something was wrong with the communication systems and he hadn't checked in. That always made his mom extra tense as well.

At dinner, Angie grew impatient about not being able to watch her normal shows. "Mommy, why do we have that reporter lady on all the time? And what are those people shouting about in front of that giant man on a horse? Is that a real horse? Why's it so big?"

"It's just a statue," Jason muttered.

"He looks *weird*."

Jason shot her an angry look. "*You're* weird."

Angie dropped her fork and opened her mouth wide. "Mommy! He said I'm weird!"

His mom walked back from the refrigerator and flicked Jason's arm as she set down the bottle of ketchup. "Be nice to your sister. It's another rally, honey. Like the one we went to with all the people."

"You look worried," said Jason. "Don't you like this one?"

"I'm cautiously optimistic," she answered. "It's wonderful to see people rallying for justice. Lord knows we need folks coming together. I just hope it stays peaceful. All that energy can do amazing things, but it can also be destructive. Sometimes when large groups get all worked up, even for a good cause, it can move in the wrong direction very quickly. I just pray that folks will know the difference tonight and that people keep cool heads. Both the protesters and the police."

His mom looked over at him. "By the way, I heard your phone buzz on the counter when you were outside earlier. It was another message from Sam."

"Why are you looking at my phone, Mom?" Jason sighed. He'd been through this a dozen times with her already. He was all done with those kids.

"Are you still not calling him back?"

"I don't want to talk about it." He set his fork down on his dinner plate, suddenly no longer hungry. "Can I be excused?"

"No, you may not," replied Angie in her bossiest little voice. Jason glared at her, but she just smirked, knowing Mom would protect her.

"Yes, but I need you to clear the dishes while I get your sister ready for her bath, please."

"Can I have bubbles in the tub this time, Mommy? I love bubbles. They're so *weird*."

"Let's see how quickly you can get changed and we'll see." Angie leaped from her seat and sprinted to the bathroom. "Don't forget about the dishes," his mom called over her shoulder as she followed Angie down the hall. "And listen for a call from your father."

"I know, Mom," he answered, a bit too loudly. "Give me a break."

"Excuse me? Would you like to try that again, mister?"

Jason sighed, but he knew better than to argue. "Yes, ma'am." Whatever his mom was feeling about the events out in Richmond, he knew it would only get him in trouble if he back-talked.

He stood next to the table and watched the newscast. It was getting dark and the crowd downtown seemed to be growing louder. Dozens of protesters flanked the reporter, most of them holding signs. Some were like the ones at the capitol rally, others said things like "No Justice, No Peace," and a few accused the police of not doing their job.

"As night descends on Richmond this evening, organizers say they intend to stay as long as it takes to get their message heard. A vigil is expected to begin at the Lee monument at ten PM. While the police presence is minimal so far, folks aren't quite sure what to expect as the evening hours grow later. The mayor is said to be discussing a curfew."

Jason turned back to the table and carried the dishes to the sink. He wondered what was going to happen out there. Would it get violent? Were people going to clash with the police? His parents didn't always agree about the best way to fight for what was right—when to talk and when to take action. When they were both in the same room, that is, which wasn't often.

STEVEN K. SMITH

His phone buzzed in his pocket. His heart jumped, and for an instant Jason thought it might be his dad, but DeShawn's name was on the screen. He contemplated not answering, but did anyway. "Hey."

"We're coming to pick you up, cuz." DeShawn sounded excited.

"Pick me up? For what?"

"Haven't you seen the news? We're heading to Richmond, and you're coming with us."

Jason struggled for an answer. "Richmond? Tonight? I can't do that."

DeShawn laughed. "Don't you wanna be a part of history? Weren't you just telling me about visiting Granny Foster? Going on about how she was part of the movement, about equality, civil rights, all that stuff?"

"Yeah, but—"

"Think about it, Jay. Where do you want to tell *your* grandchildren you were when all this was going down? Sitting home with your momma reading a book like a good boy, or out there marching with your brothers and sisters and making a difference?"

DeShawn had a way of getting Jason's head turned all around. "You know Mom's not going to let me do that..."

"She'll get over it. It's easier to get forgiveness than permission." DeShawn was quiet for a moment. "Besides, think about what your dad would do. You know he'd be out there. Think about it. I'll be there in ten minutes."

Jason knew he shouldn't go. But what DeShawn said

was true. If there was a push for justice, sometimes you had to fight for it. Leaders like Dr. King, Malcom X, Rosa Parks, even President Obama—all the people Mom was always bugging him to read about—they didn't change things by just sitting around. They acted. He wished his dad was home more than ever. He thought about trying to call him now, to talk to him about everything that was happening, but it was getting too late in his time zone and the satellite was probably still down.

He thought back to what his mom had said about Sam's message. The brothers had called several times over the past couple of weeks trying to talk, but he hadn't answered. He was done talking. They had made it plenty clear where they stood at the rally. No matter how well-meaning they might have seemed initially, they'd never be able to understand how it was. If Black folk wanted a better world, they had to fight for it. The only way to make the change was to do it themselves.

He pictured Sam again at the capitol rally talking to those bikers with the Confederate flags and shook his head. Then he picked up his phone and sent DeShawn a text before he could think about it any further.

Come pick me up. I'm in.

CHAPTER TWENTY-ONE

J ason sat in the back seat of DeShawn's car as they drove along the highway. Brennan and Antoine, the two other guys with them, were getting antsy as the lights on the buildings of Richmond grew closer. They turned off the ramp from the highway, soon cruising past some old-looking homes with front porches all lit up nice. As they drove further into the city, more and more people were walking in groups along the sidewalks. At the intersections, Jason peered down the cross-streets and saw larger crowds gathering and holding signs. But DeShawn kept driving, and soon the street traffic thinned out.

"Isn't the protest back there?" Jason asked finally when it didn't seem like they were going to stop.

Brennan chuckled next to him, red hair sticking out around the corners of his hat. A haunting grin flashed across his pale face like he was a ghost lurking in the shadows. He reached underneath the seat and pulled a wooden baseball bat from the floorboards.

"What are you going to do with that?" asked Jason.

"We're gonna stir things up, whatcha think?" Brennan flexed his grip on the bat handle like he was getting ready to step up to the plate at a ball game. "Hey, DeShawn, what did you tell your little cuz here, that we were going to a prayer meeting?"

"That's right," said Antione from the passenger seat. "It'll be easy pickins downtown if you ask me."

"Relax, Jay's cool." DeShawn glanced up at the rearview mirror. "Right, cuz?"

Jason felt his chest tighten as DeShawn's eyes met his. He didn't know what to say. He was stuck there in the car with them. If they were trying to make him nervous, it was working. "Yeah, sure, I'm cool."

DeShawn slowed the car when the road turned bumpy as they drove over cobblestones. The neighborhood they were in was a mix of stores and restaurants, but most of the windows were dark, like everything was closed. There was little traffic and Jason didn't see anyone out walking around. They turned down an alley and parked behind an old brick warehouse that was now trendy loft apartments.

DeShawn glanced at the others in the car and nodded. "Let's do this."

Jason hadn't been to Richmond very often, so he didn't know his way around. But he could see that this wasn't where they'd been for the rally by the state capitol.

He was pretty sure the protest he'd thought they were joining was back where they'd passed the crowds by the Confederate monuments.

As they stepped from the car, Jason saw Brennan slip the bat inside his loose jacket. Antione scanned the empty sidewalks, holding a dark, canvas bundle under his arm.

Jason moved next to his cousin. "What are we doing here, DeShawn? I thought we were going to march in the protest. I don't like this."

DeShawn grinned. "Nah, man. Here's the thing. We're gonna stage our own little protest, cuz. While everyone's focus is on the monuments, where do you think their focus ain't? Don't worry, you'll get a piece for yourself. We gotta show them who's in charge, you know what I mean? Marching down some street won't hit 'em where it counts. You gotta go for the wallet."

"Enough talking, let's do this," Brennan called back.

"Man up now, Jay." DeShawn tapped him on the chest with his fist. Before Jason could argue any more, DeShawn slipped past him to join Brennan and Antione up the street.

Jason felt like he was going to throw up. What was he even doing here? He pictured his mom getting Angie ready for bed. He'd lied again and said he was going to play ball. What if she found out that the gym was closed and that he wasn't with the other guys from the team? She hated it when he hung out with DeShawn in the first place. She definitely wouldn't be happy about Jason going with him to Richmond for the protest.

Worse still, they weren't even at the protest. They were here on this dark street, about to do who knows what. While his dad might have agreed with standing shoulder to shoulder with other brothers at the protest, he'd never support violence or destruction.

Jason shook his head. He couldn't just stand there. He'd get stopped by the cops for sure—a lone Black kid wandering around downtown at night. He watched the others disappear up the street. He cursed silently and started jogging. "Yo, wait up."

Jason rounded the corner to the sound of breaking glass and the shrill ringing of an alarm. Antoine was posting watch against the building. Brennan stepped over scattered broken glass, his bat in hand, as DeShawn kicked around the edges of what used to be a store window with his boot. Antione tossed them the canvas bundle, which DeShawn shook out to reveal two over-sized duffle bags.

Jason stood frozen. They were robbing a store? His eyes glanced up at the sign above the storefront. "Treads, since 1982." The name was emblazoned in red letters. He recognized it as a designer shoe store.

He scanned the street in both directions, but things were still quiet. It was a miracle that nobody had come by yet, but the alarm had to be connected to the police. Sure, he hadn't known what they were planning, but he was there and an accomplice. What did Mom call it?

Guilty by association? His dad's face flashed through his mind, but he pushed it away as tears quickly formed in his eyes.

"Oh, score!" Brennan exclaimed from inside.

"Guys, come on," said Antione. "Time to roll."

DeShawn emerged a few moments later with a stuffed bag draped over his shoulder. "Relax, man, there's no one coming. They're all tied up at the protests." He nodded confidently at Jason.

Brennan walked out behind him, his feet crunching against the broken glass. He lifted a pair of bright yellow high-tops from his bag. "Check it out. These are smoking, boy. This is what I'm talking about."

Jason stared at his cousin and shook his head. "Why are you doing this?"

"Like Robin Hood, Jay. The have-nots takin' from the haves. Don't look so sad, cuz. It's all good. I told you I'll give you a pair."

"What color you want, kid?" asked Brennan. "You can have one from my bag."

DeShawn waved up the sidewalk. "Come on. Let's go."

Jason took a final glance back at Treads. He wondered if they'd ever been robbed since they'd opened in 1982. Who owned the store? What would happen to the people that worked there? Would it put them out of business? Would everyone lose their jobs? Maybe they had insurance—he wasn't sure how that worked, but it seemed like a store would have such a thing.

PICTURES AT THE PROTEST

The pit in his stomach grew larger. The alarm was throbbing through his brain like a jackhammer. He closed his eyes, feeling like he could puke at any moment.

This wasn't him. This wasn't right. He didn't want any part of this. Suddenly he knew he had to leave, and he needed to do it right now.

"Hey, come on, cuz. Let's go," DeShawn called.

Jason didn't answer. He turned and walked away from them in the opposite direction from the car.

"Yo, Jay, where are you going?" DeShawn called out again. "Are you nuts?"

"Forget it man, just leave him. We gotta jet," Antione warned.

"Whatever, you're on your own then, man. Don't blame me," DeShawn called, his voice fading as he turned the corner.

Jason didn't look back, he just kept walking steadily across the intersection.

Then he saw the red and blue lights.

CHAPTER TWENTY-TWO

T he flashing, colored lights appeared out of nowhere. They reflected off the glass storefronts and the windows of the warehouses, piercing the darkness. For an instant, Jason froze, but then he bolted underneath a doorway awning away from any streetlamps. He pressed against the warm brick, trying to become part of the shadows as a police cruiser came up over the ridge. It roared past, bouncing hard over the cobblestones.

Jason thought his heart was going to beat right out of his chest. He couldn't breathe. His mind spun with a thousand questions: Had they seen him? Were they responding to the store alarm? Would the police stop DeShawn as he drove away? What would they do to him if they caught him? What would his mom say?

The cop car drove out of sight and the street once again fell into a quiet, hazy darkness. His ears were ringing, but Jason couldn't recall if the car's siren had been blaring or if it was still from the security alarm in Treads. The cops hadn't seen him. At least, he didn't think they had.

He had to get moving. He was a sitting duck just standing there a couple blocks from the store if they did a sweep of the neighborhood.

Jason pushed away from the building and started walking. He wanted to sprint. He wanted to run faster than he'd ever run, letting his legs carry him all the way back home to Farmville.

But he knew he couldn't. It was at least sixty miles to get home, and running anywhere would just draw more attention. The first thing the police would look for was a young Black kid sprinting through a dark neighborhood near a robbery.

He scanned the streets as he went, keeping an eye out for more police cars, but he didn't see any. Maybe DeShawn was right about the cops being too distracted with the protests. He tried to look like he belonged and keep breathing as he walked steadily up the street.

Where was he even going? He pulled out his phone and hesitated.

Should he call his mom? That was probably the right thing to do, but somehow he didn't feel ready. Not yet. He again considered trying to reach his dad, but he didn't want to disturb his sleep. He needed to be rested for whatever challenge faced him in the morning with his life on the line.

Jason remembered the reason he thought they were going downtown in the first place—the protest. He thought it was by the avenue with the monuments. He needed time to think. Right now, nothing made sense. The map on his phone showed he was nearly two miles away from the Lee monument the woman on the news had mentioned. If he hustled, he bet he could make the protest in thirty minutes. Suddenly, walking with others who were fighting for justice seemed like where he needed to be.

* * *

DEREK SHOOK his head wearily as the closing credits of the home improvement show flashed on the TV screen in the family room. "Isn't it enough that I've been working out on the deck all week? We have to watch other people do it on TV now too?"

Their dad chuckled. He'd picked that episode specifically since they'd been demonstrating the proper technique for building and staining a new deck. "I thought you might get some good tips from the experts."

"I gave him some tips from the ground," said Sam. "He didn't want them."

"He said from the *experts*, Sam," Derek grumbled. "Like the ones who'll actually climb a ladder, not just look up at it."

"How do you think you get to be an expert at anything?" Mom asked. "By lots of practice."

"Painting a deck isn't near the top of my list of things I want to become an expert on, Mom."

"Lists have a way of changing as you get older, son," said Dad, laughing. "Check back with me in ten or fifteen years when you have a home of your own to maintain."

"Uh-huh." Derek stood and stretched his arms up to the ceiling and yawned. "Maybe I'll just rent."

A news flash cut into the middle of the first commercial. A reporter was broadcasting live from Monument Avenue with large crowds of protesters standing behind her and marching along the street.

"That's a lot of people," said Derek. "Why didn't we go to that rally? It looks more exciting."

Sam's mind flashed back to seeing Mad Dog and the Ghosts at the capitol. "I think I've had enough protests for a while."

A phone rang on the table next to the couch. The boys both lunged for it, but Sam reached it first. "Oh, it's yours, Dad."

"But you never get calls." Derek glanced over at Mom. "Think he has a secret admirer?"

She pretended to be shocked and raised her eyebrows. "No comment."

"Just give me the phone, please, boys," Dad said.

Sam glanced at the screen as he handed it over. It showed Caitlin's dad's name, which was even more unusual.

"Hello?" Dad answered. "Oh, hi, Adam. Is everything okay?" He listened for a moment and then glanced up at the clock on the mantle. "What? Oh, no..."

Sam looked back at his mom and could already see the concern on her face. Dad and Mr. Murphy were friends, and sometimes the two sets of parents did things together, but it was unusual for them to talk in the evenings.

"Sure. We can do that. We'll head out now." Dad looked back at them and nodded. "No worries. It's not a problem. Yep. Thanks, Adam."

"What's wrong, honey?" Mom asked quickly.

"That was Adam Murphy."

"We know that, Dad," said Sam. "What did he want?"

Derek folded his arms and gave Sam a condescending look. "How many times have I tried to explain it to you, Sam? The guy is supposed to call the girl's father for permission, not the other way around."

Sam threw a couch pillow at him. "Very funny."

Dad shook his head. "It's a serious matter, actually."

"What's wrong?" Mom asked again.

"Well, Adam just got a call from Shanelle Thomas. It seems that Jason took a ride with his cousin into Richmond to join the protests without telling her."

"What?" exclaimed Sam.

Derek ran closer to the television. "Hey, maybe we can see him on the news."

"I'm not clear on what exactly happened," Dad continued, "but he somehow got left behind. She's got her daughter already asleep there at home and Farmville is more than an hour away, so she called Caitlin's dad to see if he could drive over and pick Jason up."

"Is he going to?" asked Sam. "And why'd he call you?"

Sam's dad reached down and pulled on his shoes. "Well, apparently Adam's up in Manassas tonight for work, so he asked if we can go instead."

Sam held his breath. It had been almost two weeks since his phone conversation with Jason—which hadn't been much of a conversation in the first place. He'd made it pretty clear he didn't want to talk to them. But now his dad was going to drive downtown in the middle of the protest and pick him up?

"Oh, the poor boy. He must be scared all by himself," said Mom.

Dad nodded and walked to the hallway. "You're likely right."

Derek turned from the TV with an excited look on his face. Sam tried to catch his attention and mouth the word "no," but Derek looked right past him. "We're coming with you."

Sam knew he needed to intervene. "He won't want to talk to us."

Derek frowned at him. "Jason barely knows Dad, Sam. We can't send him alone. Talk about awkward."

"Are you sure it's safe for the boys to come with you?" Mom asked.

"It sounds like he needs us," replied Dad. "If the boys want to come, we'll be careful."

"Does that mean yes?" asked Derek.

Dad nodded. "Sam, you've been looking for a way to show Jason how you really feel about being friends. Maybe this is your opportunity."

Sam stared back at the people marching on the TV. He was getting tired of his dad being right. He let out a long breath. "Fine. Let's go."

CHAPTER TWENTY-THREE

"**D**o you think the protest covers all of Monument Avenue?" asked Derek.

"I think it's focused up near the Lee monument," Dad answered, "but it looked like a sizable crowd in the news video."

They slowed as they drove into the neighborhood Sam remembered was called the Fan. Grand houses lined both sides of the street. The lots were small, but the homes looked fancy and old. Living in this part of the city would probably be a lot different from living near the woods and the creek that he was used to in the suburbs.

Even though it was after ten o'clock, groups of people were streaming steadily along the sidewalks in both directions, sometimes even spilling out onto the road next to the parked cars at the curb. The few times that Sam had been downtown at night had usually been for a college basketball game. There were always scores of people on the sidewalks heading for the arena on game night, but there weren't any games downtown tonight, and the crowds were bigger than he remembered.

As they turned toward Monument Avenue, he wondered how it would feel to be walking around alone at night. Sure, there might be a lot of other people, but it seemed like it would still be a little scary by himself. Jason must have come downtown with DeShawn for the protest, even though he knew his mom wouldn't like it. Jason had told them before that he sometimes hung out with his cousin against his better judgement.

He'd also said that he did it because family was complicated, which was certainly true. Despite all Derek's craziness and annoying habits, he was connected to Sam, for better or for worse. But why Jason would now be alone after arriving with DeShawn was a mystery. It would be a cold move, even for DeShawn, to just leave his cousin here with no ride, over an hour from home.

"The Lee monument is just a few blocks away. Why don't you text Jason and see exactly where he is?" Dad pointed toward the curb. "Derek, tell me if you see any open parking spots along that side of the street."

"He's not going to like it," replied Sam, typing a brief message into his phone. "Do you think his mom even told him we're coming?"

"I don't know, but we can't leave him here in the city by himself." Dad slowed the car to a crawl on the next block.

"There's a spot. That guy's leaving," called Derek as red taillights pulled out in front of them.

Sam felt his phone buzz in his hand as Dad pulled even with a parked car and then eased backward, cutting the wheel sharply toward the curb to parallel park in the open spot.

What do you mean you're here? Jason replied.

We're picking you up. Your mom asked us.

"What did he say?" asked Derek.

The phone was dark for a few seconds, but then it showed Jason was writing something. "He says he's on Monument and Mulberry," Sam read. "Is that close?"

"About six blocks from here," said Dad. "Tell him to stay put. We'll come to him."

"Aren't we going to drive there?" asked Sam.

"No, let's walk," Derek said quickly. "I want to be out there experiencing the protest. It won't feel the same in the car."

Dad looked out at the busy street. "It's going to be hard to find another parking spot much closer. Walking probably would be easier."

"Maybe we should have been here anyway, helping support social justice, don't you think, Dad?" asked Derek as they stepped out onto the sidewalk. "I mean, just like at the capitol."

Dad nodded. "You could be right, son. But let's try to stay together and keep our eyes open."

They turned down the next side street and walked until they reached Monument Avenue. The air was warm, and Sam could feel the tension surging through the crowd. The police seemed to have blocked off the road from vehicles, and a long sea of people walked right down the middle of the street, many of them holding signs and banners. Others stood in the grassy median between the two lanes of the avenue, cheering and holding more signs.

The news had said that similar events in other cities had led to clashes between protestors and the authorities. Everyone here seemed calm at the moment, but Sam had heard these types of situations could turn ugly fast. "Do you think it's going to stay peaceful?"

"I hope so," said Dad. "There's a lot of frustration that's built up along this avenue over the decades. Many people are angry and feel like their voices haven't been heard. Sometimes when all those feelings get bottled up for so long, they have nowhere to go, so they explode. But we have to hope things can be dealt with before they get to that point."

Sam glanced around at the crowd and the police stationed on the side streets and cringed. As much as he wanted to support what was right, he didn't want to be caught up in the middle of an explosion.

"Are we almost there?"

"I think Mulberry is the next block," said Dad. "Ask him which corner he's on and what he's wearing."

"Gray Nike T-shirt," Sam reported after getting Jason's reply.

"Oh, that will be easy to find," said Derek, sarcastically.

They moved closer to the end of the block and scanned the crowd from the sidewalk. Sam looked on the far side of the street where the darkness mixed with the streetlights to create a murky haze. His eyes landed on Jason's face. He was staring in the other direction. He hadn't seen them yet.

Sam pointed across the street. "There he is. Come on."

"Careful, Sam!" Derek pulled him back just as a bicycle flashed right past them going the wrong way. Sam felt a surge of adrenaline and shook his head. He should have looked more closely. It wasn't the first time he'd almost been walloped when stepping too fast off the curb on this road.

"Why don't I go first," said Derek, checking both ways this time. They stepped through a break in the crowd toward the other side of the street. Jason didn't see them until they were right next to him.

"Hey," Derek called.

Jason looked wary, but he also seemed relieved.

Dad leaned down so he could be heard over the crowd noise. "Are you okay, son?"

Jason nodded. "Yeah. My mom called you?"

"She did," replied Sam. "Well, she called Caitlin's dad first, but he's out of town. So he called us."

"What are you doing out here by yourself?" asked Derek.

Jason looked off into the distance. "It's a long story."

"Ready to get out of here?" asked Sam.

"Yeah," Jason replied, not hesitating this time.

"Wait for it…" said Derek, holding his finger in the air as he glanced at their dad.

"Let's all stay together," Dad said on cue, not catching the joke as he looked back across the street.

Sam laughed.

"He says that a lot?" asked Jason.

"It's like clockwork," said Derek.

As they moved back up Monument Avenue toward the car, Sam walked next to Jason. But he was scared to say too much. Instead, Sam looked ahead several blocks and saw the Lee monument rising above the street, surrounded by another swell in the crowd. Dad stepped to the corner and turned to cross the street toward the car. Derek held up his hand. "Can't we walk by the Lee monument first? I mean, we're all the way down here. Can't we see it?"

"I think maybe Jason wants to get home," Dad replied, looking over to see his response.

Jason shook his head. "I'd like to see it, actually. I mean, if you don't mind. I got mixed up in the crowds and walked in the wrong direction. So I haven't seen it yet either."

Dad checked the time, but nodded. "Okay, just for a few minutes."

Sam felt anxious as they walked closer. He didn't know what to expect, but he felt conspicuous, like they were walking in on someone else's event. When he looked closer, he realized that the crowd was almost equally mixed. It was cool to see young and old people as well as people from different races all walking together; all realizing the need for change.

They crossed against the flow of protesters on the sidewalk and moved to the grassy area in the center of the avenue. Sam had seen the statue several times before during the daytime, but somehow the sheer size of it caught him off guard as they approached through the crowd. While they'd driven by the monument in the past, Sam didn't know if they'd ever stood this close to it.

He glanced over at Jason staring up at the scene and wondered what he was thinking. "It's so big," he muttered.

A wide banner for racial justice was draped across the top of the platform just below Lee's horse, and dozens of messages had been spray-painted on the lower sections of the stone. Some of them weren't legible, but some were messages of peace while others were angry curses about the police.

It was weird seeing the giant statue in that condition. There was no way to stand there and not sense the enormity of the situation, but Sam didn't know exactly how to feel. Was it wrong to deface a historic monument that had stood for over a hundred years, or was it bringing an end to a reminder of Richmond's slavery-ridden past and giving a voice to those who hadn't had one?

As they stood watching, a light shot out from one

side of the grassy circle around the monument. It projected faint images of faces over the wide, stone foundation beneath the horse.

"Look at that," called Derek. Sam realized that a man was sitting across the circle with a laptop connected to a projector. "Who are those faces?"

"I think they're people who were killed or faced injustice," said Dad quietly.

Sam glanced back at Jason. Sam thought he saw a tear slip down his face, but Jason wiped it away quickly so Sam couldn't be sure.

Jason turned and caught Sam's gaze, his face full of emotion. "It's not right, you know," he said in barely over a whisper.

Sam bit his lip. He knew he needed to say something. He wanted to say what was in his heart, but he felt like every time he tried to explain, the words just didn't come out right. A weight was building in his chest. He opened his mouth, but nothing came out. It was like the walls were closing in.

Then he did something without hardly thinking about it. He reached his arm out and slowly draped it over Jason's shoulder. He felt Jason freeze for an instant with uncertainty, but then he let out a long breath and seemed to relax.

For several minutes, none of them spoke. They all just stood there watching the faces flash across the monument, stark contrasts to the dark shadow of General Lee astride his mount above.

CHAPTER TWENTY-FOUR

S tudents seemed to be gearing up for move-in day as Sam, Caitlin, Derek, and Jason walked between the buildings at VCU. Caitlin had spoken to Natalie Roberts on the phone and given her their update about the picture. It was Natalie's idea that they come by in person and that Jason join them. He seemed legitimately eager to come, and this time he got his mom's permission.

"So you're not in trouble or anything?" asked Derek.

Jason sighed. "Oh, I'm in trouble, don't worry. My mom woke my dad up in Afghanistan when she found out where I was. He called this morning and gave me a long talk. I'm totally grounded, but my mom made an exception since this tied into the picture with Granny Foster. She said it's something positive I can do with my time since I won't be hanging out with DeShawn anytime soon. She and my aunt are meeting with his lawyer this morning."

"Do you think he's going to jail?" asked Sam. Jason had told them on the way home from Monument Avenue what had happened with his cousin at the shoe store. It was after midnight when they'd dropped Jason home back in Farmville, so they hadn't stayed to talk after he had gotten in the door. But the next day, Mrs. Thomas had called to thank them again. She shared what Jason hadn't known in the car, that DeShawn and his two buddies were picked up by the police just as they reached their car. It was tough explaining why they had two bags filled with stolen shoes.

"With his record, he's likely going away somewhere." Jason shook his head. "I just can't believe how close that came to being me too. I keep waking up with nightmares."

"But you didn't really do anything," said Derek.

Jason shook his head. "I should never have been there in the first place. I should have said no. I knew better."

"At least you made the right decision the second time," said Caitlin. "That counts for something."

"I guess."

"They didn't have you on the security camera or anything?" asked Derek.

Jason shook his head. "I don't think so. I got lucky that I didn't walk into the store, and DeShawn told my aunt that he didn't tell the police about me being along for the ride. I feel terrible for the owner of the store, though. They have to repair a lot of damage."

"At least they got the shoes back," said Derek.

"I'm glad you're safe," said Sam, stopping at the steps outside the library building. He was about to say something more, but hesitated, pulling at the edge of his T-shirt.

"What?" asked Jason.

Sam took a deep breath. "I just wanted to say again that I'm sorry for not saying something before with the bikers. I should have."

Jason nodded. "You're right. You should have. Guys like that are bad news." He sighed and gazed across the street. "But I guess I've proven it's easy to make mistakes. Maybe what we do next is the important part, you know?"

"Yeah." Sam grinned, relieved to have cleared the air. He pointed to the entrance. "Ready to go in?"

"Definitely." Jason laughed. "This is getting awkward."

They caught up with Caitlin and Derek just outside Natalie's office. After Jason and Derek were introduced, everyone took seats around the table.

"Thanks for finding this picture of my granny," Jason said. "My mom really appreciated it. And so did I."

"It's my favorite part of this project," Natalie answered, "seeing families make connections from the past. We have plenty of other pictures if you four are interested in doing some more sleuthing. I know a talented team when I see one. I'd be a fool to let you all off the hook." She smiled at Jason. "What do you think?"

He glanced at the others. "Well, I didn't really do anything. It was just my granny, is all. I'm not sure I would be much help."

"Nonsense," Natalie replied. "You live right in Farmville. It would be mighty convenient for you to work with the folks at the Moton Museum, Longwood University, and the county records office on these pictures. You'd be our man on the scene."

"Oh, that reminds me," Caitlin blurted. "I'd meant to tell all of them what we found."

"You want to tell the guy at the county records office?" asked Derek. "He was kind of strange."

Caitlin laughed. "No, I might skip him, but Tiffany and Mrs. Baines for sure. I'm sure they'd want to know that we found Miriam Cartwright."

"They most definitely would," agreed Natalie.

Sam tapped Jason's shoulder. "What do you think? Wanna help us? Derek isn't even interested most of the time, so it wouldn't be too bad."

Derek shot him a look. "Hey, I'm sitting right here, you know."

Jason laughed. "Why not? It sounds fun."

"Excellent," said Natalie. "I'd hoped that you'd continue on, so I've already made copies of the rest of the mystery pictures for your files. Feel free to get started on whichever ones you'd like."

"Maybe we could split them up and make it a competition," suggested Derek. "You know, with a big prize to the winner."

Caitlin rolled her eyes. "Or we could just work together and have fun connecting with history."

Derek sighed. "Or we could do that."

"So, do we have to get matching T-shirts and stuff now?" Jason asked.

Sam grinned. "No, you just need to learn the secret handshakes and get your decoder ring. Do you want blue or yellow?"

"And we'll introduce you to the crime dog and ride in the mystery van tomorrow." Caitlin laughed.

Derek told Natalie about how they'd been at the protest by the Lee monument. "What's going to happen with all those Confederate monuments, do you think?"

"I don't know," Natalie answered. "It seems like things are going to change."

"It would be weird without them there on Monument Avenue," said Sam.

"You sound like my sister," said Jason.

"Do you think it's good for them to be removed?" Caitlin asked.

Natalie thought for a moment and then nodded. "I've had mixed feelings about that over the years. I used to think of them as being important to Virginia's history, and that simply adding context and historical markers would be a good way to teach and educate."

"But now you don't think so?" asked Sam.

Natalie nodded. "I think we're too far past that now. There's a fine line between learning from mistakes in the past and honoring them. A lot of folks are starting to realize that those statues were adding to the problem. They are part of the 'Lost Cause' interpretation of the Civil War that too often discounts the horrors of slavery."

"I don't know how anyone could forget about that," said Caitlin.

"History can be peculiar like that sometimes. Things stay the same for decades, and then suddenly change kicks into high gear. It can move like a swell in the ocean to where it's almost inevitable." Natalie smiled at Jason. "Just like back in Farmville during the protests. Those leaders tried to block the students' efforts, but there was no stopping the tide from coming."

"I'm glad you found that picture of my granny," said Jason. "I'm proud of her."

"You should be," said Natalie. "What she did took a lot of courage."

"Just like Barbara Johns," Caitlin added. "I'll bet neither one of them knew if they could actually make a difference. They had so much working against them. But they tried anyway."

"Massive Resistance seems like it would have been a lot of work," said Sam. "I can't understand why people would have fought so hard against treating people fairly."

Natalie leaned back in her chair. "Sometimes people are afraid. Sometimes it's ignorance. Sometimes it's just how they've been raised. But things are slowly changing with each generation. More slowly than they should, but they're changing."

Sam thought about how Mr. Haskins' generation was a lot different from all of their parents' attitudes, and how those opinions were even different from those of many kids his age. Who knew how things would be when he started a family someday? Discrimination might keep getting less and less, although there still seemed to be plenty of people like the Ghosts who were more interested in keeping things like the past than improving the future.

"Remember how Barbara Johns said it felt?" asked Caitlin. "Like they were reaching for the moon."

"And I keep thinking back to what it said on that monument from Thurgood Marshall," said Jason.

"Oh yeah," said Derek. "That the courts can knock down the house but can't clean up the mess, right?"

Natalie laughed. "It said that, did it?"

"I think you mean they can't build bridges," said Caitlin.

Derek shrugged. "I'm paraphrasing. You know what I mean."

Jason glanced at Sam and smiled. "The bridge-building part is up to all of us."

"Amen," said Natalie. "I think you kids are getting the idea." She glanced at Caitlin discretely. "Isn't there something else you wanted to do before you left?"

"Oh!" Caitlin's eyes widened. "I nearly forgot!" She reached down and pulled her backpack into her lap.

Sam lowered his eyebrows. "What's going on?"

Derek looked like it was taking all he had to keep a straight face. "You'll see."

Caitlin pulled two square packages wrapped in brown shipping paper from her backpack. She handed them to Natalie and then nodded back to Sam and Jason.

Sam didn't enjoy being left out of things. He turned to Jason, but he just shrugged like he was as clueless as Sam was.

Natalie gave Sam and Jason serious looks and suddenly Sam felt like he might be in trouble, although he couldn't think of what he might have done wrong. Whatever it was, Jason seemed to have done it too.

"You two both know how important this *Freedom Now* project is for so many in the community," said Natalie.

"Sure," Sam answered. "Of course."

"Yes, ma'am," said Jason.

"Well, we've been thinking that it might be nice to add some new photos to our digital collection." Her serious face turned friendly as she handed Sam and Jason each one of the two brown packages.

Sam frowned. "What is it?"

"Open it!" said Caitlin.

He glanced at Jason and shrugged. It wasn't his birthday anytime soon, but a present was a present. They both ripped back the brown paper, revealing the back of a metal frame.

"Turn it over," said Derek.

They both rotated their frames, and Sam heard Jason catch his breath at the same time that he did. His mouth dropped open in surprise as he stared down at the picture behind the glass. It was a black-and-white photo from the protest at the Lee Monument. It was taken from behind Sam and Jason as they stood next to each other, with Sam's arm draped around Jason's shoulder. The monument was in the background, the image of a projected face was shining on the base of the monument, and the hazy glow of the night was all around them.

"Wow…" said Jason.

Sam turned to Caitlin and Derek. "Where did you get this? Who took the picture?"

"Derek did," Caitlin answered.

"You were standing behind us?" asked Jason.

Derek winked at them. "I'm sneaky."

"He told me about it after you got back," said Caitlin. "And when I showed it to my dad, he had the idea of printing it up like that. Did you see the frame?"

Sam had been so surprised to see the photo that he'd barely noticed the custom detail along the edge of the frame. Along the top edge was a thin, metal decorative bridge that looked just like the High Bridge. And along the bottom was a small set of glasses frames.

"It seemed appropriate," said Derek.

"What do you think?" asked Natalie.

Sam shook his head. "I don't know what to say." He turned to Jason, who was still staring at the picture.

"These are for us to keep?" Jason asked. "For real?"

"Of course," said Caitlin.

"You're welcome," said Derek, grinning.

Sam rolled his eyes but laughed. "Thanks."

* * *

"SO, I was looking at the schedule for the new basketball season," said Derek after they'd said goodbye to Natalie and walked back out to the sidewalk. "It looks like the Knicks are coming to DC to play the Wizards in February. Maybe we could all go."

"That sounds fun," said Jason. "I think my dad might be home by then."

"Perfect," said Derek. "He can come too."

"We'll probably get crushed," said Sam.

Jason laughed. "I hope so."

"Think you'll still be grounded by then?" asked Caitlin.

"Tough to say." Jason held up the photo binder that Natalie had given them. "Hopefully, my mom will like that I'm helping you guys identify more of these pictures."

"Where do you think we should start?" asked Derek.

"Maybe Jason should pick the next one," said Caitlin.

"Sure, my granny would probably like that. I'll have a look at them all when I get home." Jason held up his frame. "This is really cool, guys. Thanks again. I can't wait to show my parents."

"We thought you'd like it," Caitlin answered. "And you get to be part of Natalie's collection."

Sam stared back down at his copy of the picture and the silhouetted outline of him and Jason watching the monument. It was a little like the pictures from the other protest—a simple captured moment—but it was churning with emotion just below the surface. He wondered if anyone might look at the photo years from now to try to better understand what was going on in his time.

Would the same problems still exist? Maybe change would remove the need for protests about discrimination and justice. As great as that sounded, he knew there always seemed to be things in the world that needed fighting for. He usually thought that meant in wars, like Jason's dad overseas, but there were a lot of wrongs to right here at home too.

He looked up at Derek and Caitlin. Sometimes even his brother surprised him. "It's perfect, guys. Thanks." Then he turned and smiled at Jason. "Thanks to you too."

Jason raised his eyebrows. "Me? For what?"

"For helping me see things a little more clearly."

Jason chuckled. "All I did was find your glasses, man."

Sam grinned. "Exactly."

CHAPTER TWENTY-FIVE

"They'd better not make us ride the junior-size cars just because Sam's here," Derek moaned as they turned off the highway. They were finally on the way to the long-promised go-kart track. Their efforts with tracking down the pictures had distracted them, and then it had rained the past two Saturdays. But now the sun was finally shining, and Derek could barely contain his plans to send Sam into the wall.

"Give me a break," Sam argued. "I'm nearly as tall as you are. Don't start making excuses for why you got beat before we even start."

"Maybe." Derek shrugged. "At least try not to lose your glasses, okay?"

"Just try not to choke on my exhaust fumes." Sam watched a motorcycle zoom by them out the window. He wondered if they ever made go-karts that drove as fast as that. The bike turned off into a parking lot up ahead at a roadside bar. His eyes caught a flash of something as they drove by, but it took a moment for his brain to register what he'd seen. "Dad, stop the car!" he shouted as it clicked in his head.

His dad pumped the brakes and glanced back at him in the rearview mirror. "What's wrong?"

Sam craned his neck to see the road behind them. "Nothing's wrong, but we need to turn around."

"Are you getting scared already about me beating you on the track?" Derek teased. "You could at least wait until we get there to chicken out."

Sam ignored him. "Sorry, I'll explain in a second, Dad, but could you please turn around and go back to that building we just passed? I need to see something."

His dad looked confused, but he shifted into the left lane and did a U-turn. "Okay, but it's only cutting into your race time."

Sam directed them into the parking lot of the place he'd seen. Dad leaned forward and peered through the windshield at the sign for the crusty-looking roadside tavern. He turned around and gave Sam a questioning look.

"You want to go here?" asked Derek. "You know, you're just slightly below the drinking age, Sam."

"What's up?" Dad asked.

Sam leaned back to get a better view of the side of the building. He needed to make sure he'd seen correctly, but it was just as he'd thought. A long row of Harleys lined the side of the building. And he'd recognize that image of a ghost over the Confederate flag anywhere.

He looked up at Dad and Derek in the front seat with a toothy grin. "So, here's the thing…" he began.

* * *

THE NOXIOUS SMELL of musty beer and cigarettes hit them as soon as they pushed open the door. The room was dimly lit and a twangy country music song played from a jukebox somewhere. A couple guys with cues stood around a pool table in the corner, and a long wooden bar was straight ahead.

Sam felt his knees weaken, but he bit his lip and pushed himself to keep going.

It had taken a lot of convincing before his dad would let him do this. He wasn't going to chicken out now. He'd pleaded his case with his dad out in the parking lot for at least ten minutes until it finally became clear that he was serious and wasn't just messing around.

It was hard to explain, but for the last few weeks, Sam had known deep down that there was something he still needed to do. When he'd glimpsed the motorcycle driving past, that feeling hit him like a freight train. He knew if he didn't act now, he would regret it for a very long time.

Dad and Derek followed behind him into the bar. That was the only way Dad had agreed to let him go in. It felt like one of those scenes in the movies where the conversations all stopped and everyone stared up at them. He felt completely out of place, but he tried to keep breathing as he scanned the room.

Derek nudged him and nodded at a corner near the pool table. Mad Dog was playing cards with two other guys. When Sam glanced behind him, his dad looked like he was contemplating pulling the plug at any moment. Even Derek seemed hesitant for a change.

But Sam knew he couldn't stop now. He ignored the pounding in his chest and willed his legs forward to the table.

A guy behind the bar held up his hand like a crossing guard. "Hey, hang on just a minute there. What are you doing in here, kid?"

Sam ignored him and kept walking toward the table in the corner.

"Hey, I'm talking to you." The man was moving around the bar when Mad Dog glanced up at the commotion. He looked pretty surprised to see Sam in there, but then he grinned and motioned to the bartender it was all right.

"Well ain't this somethin'," Mad Dog bellowed. "You are just one surprise after another lately, aren't you, little man?"

Sam swallowed hard as he stepped up to the table. "Hey." He didn't want to get caught up in too much small talk or else he'd lose his nerve for what he'd come to do.

"To what do we owe this pleasure?" Mad Dog

noticed Sam's dad and Derek by the entrance and gave them a slight wave. "Everything okay?"

"Yeah," Sam started. "Well, actually, no."

Mad Dog raised his eyebrows and pointed to an open chair. "Wanna sit down?"

Sam shook his head. "No thanks."

He took a deep breath.

"You see, something's been eating at me ever since I saw you at the capitol. I wasn't at the rally to support Southern pride or the Confederacy. I was there with my friend, Jason Thomas, and his family, to support social justice. I didn't say anything when we ran into you and Chris because, well, it was easier to just stay quiet and let you think what you wanted. But it's not true."

He paused, waiting for Mad Dog to explode, but he just stared back silently.

"I don't know why you guys are named the Confederate Ghosts, why you think that flag should keep flying, or why you showed up at the rally. I hope it's not because you think that Virginia or this country should be different for people based on where they come from or the color of their skin. I hope you don't think people like my friend Jason should be discriminated against or not have the same opportunities we do just because we were born white."

He glanced back at the door to make sure his dad and Derek were still there. He was on a roll now, but he feared a crowd of bikers might form behind him at any moment and clobber him.

"I don't mean to be rude or disrespectful. You've always been super kind and thoughtful to Caitlin, Derek, and me, and I've always liked you. But seeing you at the rally the way we did almost cost me a friend, and worse than that, it made it seem like I supported something I don't. And I just couldn't look at myself in the mirror if I didn't set things straight with you."

It felt like the room had gone deadly silent, but it was probably just his imagination. For what seemed like an eternity, Sam just stood there waiting for a reaction. His ears felt hot, like they'd turned bright red. Now that he'd said what he had, it hit him what a dangerous situation he'd put himself in.

Suddenly Mad Dog raised a heavy palm and smacked it hard against the tabletop. Sam flinched and thought maybe he'd been shot, but all his arms and legs still seemed to be connected. Mad Dog stood, leaning over the table and reaching his arm out menacingly. Sam braced himself for the big man to yell and curse at him, or maybe grab him up by the ankles and throw him across the bar.

But Mad Dog did something surprising.

Instead of reaching out to wring Sam's neck, he held out his hand. It took a moment for Sam to figure out what was happening, but then he tentatively returned the gesture and they shook.

"I respect that about you, kid," Mad Dog growled.

Sam blinked and tried to make sure he'd heard right. "Wait... you do?"

Mad Dog let out a laugh. "Sure. I've always said that a man isn't worth his salt unless he's willing to stand up for what he believes in. I admire your conviction, especially for a kid your age. It's hard for old dogs like me to change, but you've given me some things to think about."

Sam let out a long breath and slowly felt the tension releasing. He smiled back tentatively at the tall man. "Thanks."

Mad Dog nodded at the door. "Looks like some folks are waiting for you over there."

Sam turned and saw Dad and Derek with incredulous looks on their faces. He wondered if they'd been almost as nervous as he was.

"You should probably beat it before a brawl or something breaks out in here." Mad Dog chuckled. "I might need to knock a few skulls just to remind the boys I haven't lost my edge."

"Right." Sam stepped back from the table. "Okay, well, see ya."

He turned and hurried past Dad and Derek to the door, waving subtly for them to follow.

When he stepped onto the gravel in the parking lot, Sam leaned over with his hands on his knees and exhaled. He suddenly felt like he'd been holding his breath for hours.

Derek bounded out and put his hands on Sam's shoulders. "Oh my gosh! I thought you were seconds away from being a goner, Sam. It looked like he was about to body slam you."

Dad looked down at him. "Are you okay?"

Sam straightened up and nodded. "Yeah. But I'm glad that's over."

"What did you say to him?" asked Derek.

Sam grinned. "Pretty much what I told you I would say. I explained that we'd been at the rally for social justice and not to support the Confederacy. I expected him to be angry, but that's when he just shook my hand. He said he respected me standing up for my beliefs, or something like that. It's all kind of a blur."

Dad patted him on the back. "I'm proud of you, buddy."

"Thanks."

"Do you feel better?"

Sam pursed his lips and thought for a second. "Yeah. It was the right thing to do, don't you think?"

Dad laughed nervously. "It might not have been the exact route I'd have chosen, but maybe it was the best one for you." He glanced down at them knowingly. "Let's not tell Mom about this right away, okay? I'll need to pick the right time to gently explain what happened."

Sam laughed. "Sounds good. Thanks for letting me do that. I think that's the last time I want to see those guys."

"Your mom *will* like that." Dad tussled Sam's hair. "You boys both have a lot more to offer this world than hanging out with groups who tolerate spreading hate."

Derek opened the car door. "I'm with you, Dad, but are we going to ride those go-karts or not?"

Dad pulled out his keys. "As long as your brother is still up for it."

Sam grinned and slid into the car. He felt like someone had lifted an enormous weight from his shoulders. "Let's do it. But I'm going to put you right in the wall."

ACKNOWLEDGMENTS

Pictures at the Protest might be the hardest, and perhaps the most important, book I've written. I'd planned for the past year to have the next mystery book tied to Virginia's history with civil rights. I'd just begun my research when the COVID-19 pandemic hit in March 2020, and my busy slate of in-person school visits started dropping like dominoes as classrooms moved to virtual learning. A connection immediately struck me between the current events and my recent research about how schools in Prince Edward County closed to prevent desegregation. I thought the present-day situation might help catch readers' attention and bring even more appreciation and visibility to the important and tragic events from nearly sixty years ago and the ongoing struggle for justice and equality.

I was drawn in by the brave 16-year-old named Barbara Johns, who stood up and challenged the unfair conditions at her school in 1951. Her actions helped spark court cases that became part of the landmark 1954 US Supreme Court decision in *Brown v. Board of Education*. My research included learning more about Jim Crow, Massive Resistance, other key court decisions like *Green vs. Co. School Board of New Kent*, Richmond's historic Jackson Ward, Evergreen Cemetery, and the Civil Rights Memorial at the Virginia State Capitol. The striking images from VCU's *Freedom Now* project of student protesters along Main Street Farmville in 1963 and the real unidentified "mystery photos" struck me as a fascinating element for the plot.

As I explored the civil rights movement of the 1950s and 60s, the summer of 2020 was exploding with protests and unrest over police brutality and calls for social justice in Richmond and across the country. Many of the Confederate statues on Richmond's Monument Avenue started coming down. Like many, I struggled to make sense of what was happening. As a white, middle-class male who grew up in New Jersey, I was less familiar with some of the specific history of Virginia's civil rights. I have not experienced the struggle that many African Americans have endured and face on a daily basis. But remaining uneducated about a topic is often the easiest way to "innocently" ignore injustice. As an author and citizen, I attempted to listen, empathize, and learn as much truth as possible from my research and discussions with those who have faced many of these challenges head-on. While my efforts are by no means complete, they included several Zoom calls with some of the first students to desegregate New Kent County public schools during Freedom of Choice, conversations and tours with staff from the education team at the Robert Russa Moton Museum, Richmond's Black History Museum, the National Park Service at the Maggie Walker House, the Enrichmond Foundation at Evergreen Cemetery, and a wide range of instructive articles, books, and films, some of which I've listed below.

As with a lot of the topics I've researched, there was enough content to fill many different books and story-lines. My goal in *The Virginia Mysteries* series is not to be political, controversial, or to tell someone else's story, but rather to present ideas that are thought-provoking, exciting, and educational for young readers, families, and classrooms. Some may take offense in this book at where I drew the line on certain topics and issues, believing I went too far or not far enough, but I attempted to show characters with different perspectives while presenting dialogue and interactions as truthfully as possible. Mad Dog DeWitt and the Confederate Ghosts first appeared in the third book of this series, *Ghosts of Belle Isle*, and again briefly in books five and eight. I was becoming increasingly aware and uncomfortable that their commitment to "southern pride" and political views that were never explained. This book seemed an appropriate time to call them to account while challenging the young protagonists (and perhaps readers) to examine their own viewpoints and what they're willing to stand for. In a country often more divided than ever, I pray that we might all look for opportunities to speak out against hate and injustice, and lean more toward what we hold in common than what pulls us apart. Thank you for your grace with my own imperfect attempt to better learn and navigate these waters, both on and off these pages.

Resources that aided my research in writing this book included (note many are intended for older audiences): *The Girl from the Tar Paper School: Barbara Rose Johns and the Advent of the Civil Rights Movement* by Teri Kanefield; *Something Must Be Done About Prince Edward County* by Kristen Green; *The Road to Healing* by Ken Woodley; *Stamped: Racism, Antiracism, and You* by Jason Reynolds and Ibram X. Kendi; *The Sin of Racism* by Timothy Keller; *We Face the Dawn* by Margaret Edds; *Compassion & Conviction* by Justin Giboney, Michael Wear, and Chris Butler; *The Politics of Annexation* by John V. Moeser and Rutledge M. Dennis; *Selma* (2014); *Just Mercy* (2019); *13th* (2017); *Loving* (2016); Virginia Museum of History & Culture; Black History Museum & Cultural Center of Virginia; Encyclopedia Virginia; Robert Russa Moton Museum.

Many thanks to those who shared insights, instructed, and taught me invaluable pieces of history, and provided feedback on my manuscript, including: Alice Campbell, Trendell Clark, Sylvia Hathaway, Lana Krumwiede, Peg Noctor, Faithe Norrell, Anthony Ntumy, Kenn Otey, Genifer Ross, Jim Shadoian, Cainan Townsend, Camilla Tramuel, and Larry Woodson. As always, I could not do any of this without the love and support of my family. Thanks to my wife Mary, my first reader and frequent sounding board, Aaron, Josh, and Matthew. My publishing team continues to make things run smoothly—thanks to Dane at eBook Launch for another amazing cover, Kim Sheard for her edits and dealing with my tight deadlines, Stephanie Parent for proofreading, Tom McElroy in advance for his audiobook narration of all the previous books in the series, and my enthusiastic advance reader team and everyone's help spreading the news.

Finally, thank you to all my readers for allowing me to pursue my dreams and making this surprising gig of making up stories a reality.

ABOUT THE AUTHOR

Steven K. Smith is the author of *The Virginia Mysteries*, *Brother Wars*, and *Final Kingdom* series for middle grade readers. He lives with his wife, three sons, and a golden retriever in Richmond, Virginia.

For more information, visit:

www.stevenksmith.net

steve@myboys3.com

ALSO BY STEVEN K. SMITH

MYBOYS3 PRESS SUPPORTS

CHAT

Sam, Derek, and Caitlin aren't the only kids who crave adventure. Whether near woods in the country or amidst tall buildings and the busy urban streets of a city, every child needs exciting ways to explore his or her imagination, excel at learning and have fun.

A portion of the proceeds from *The Virginia Mysteries* series will be donated to the great work of **CHAT (Church Hill Activities & Tutoring)**. CHAT is a nonprofit group that works with kids in the Church Hill neighborhood of inner-city Richmond, Virginia.

To learn more about CHAT, including opportunities to volunteer or contribute financially, visit **www. chatrichmond.org.**

DID YOU ENJOY PICTURES AT THE PROTEST?

WOULD YOU ... REVIEW?

Online reviews are crucial for indie authors like me. They help bring credibility and make books more discoverable by new readers. No matter where you purchased your book, if you could take a few moments and give an honest review at one of the following websites, I'd be so grateful.

Amazon.com
BarnesandNoble.com
Goodreads.com

Thank you and thanks for reading!

Steve

CPSIA information can be obtained
at www.ICGtesting.com
Printed in the USA
LVHW041255201220
674660LV00002B/2

9 781947 881280